Dreams do come True!

Natalia Reis

HER REAL Man

RESCUE ME COLLECTION
NATALIA REIS

For information, contact the publisher, Hot Tree Publishing.
www.hottreepublishing.com

EDITING: HOT TREE EDITING
FORMATTING: RMGraphX
COVER DESIGNER: SOXSATIONAL COVER ART

ISBN-13: 978-1-925655-50-6

10 9 8 7 6 5 4 3 2 1

More From *Natalina*

FANTASY ROMANCE
DESERT JEWEL
SNOW JEWEL (DESERT JEWEL #2)

CONTEMPORARY ROMANCE
LOVE YOU ALWAYS
BLIND MAGIC
HER REAL MAN

GAY ROMANCE
LAVENDER FIELDS

To all firefighters, here and abroad.
You're real life heroes.
Thank you.

Real Men and Chicken

Ana

What was I thinking? The bulging muscles, the tattoos, the profusion of hairy body surfaces…. I was so tired of the super-buff, testosterone-oozing, romantic hero I'd been writing about for years. Yes, I was a stereotype: the lonely thirty-something woman who wrote those larger than life (and larger than trucks) male characters so she could retreat into her fantasy world and feel less lonely. Except I wasn't into that kind of man at all. Like with everything else in my life, I liked moderation in the muscle realm. If a guy looked like he had managed to somehow inflate air into his biceps and pecs, I wasn't interested. If the width of his legs had more in common with a tree than actual human limbs, scratch him off my list. If he was so built he could barely move without looking like the Pillsbury Doughboy, no way in hell!

I like my men slim with well-defined muscles, little to no facial hair—what's up with all those Abe Lincoln beards anyway?—and human features. Not someone who is as beautiful as Legolas in *The Lord of the Rings*. I have nothing against beauty, but let's be honest. Do I really want a man who is prettier than me?

However, my readers love the Hulk-of-a-Man, all hard muscle and features so perfect you have to wonder if they're real. So, I write them in my stories.

For once I wanted to write a book about a real man. *Why can't I? I can, right? Who exactly is holding me back?* Feeling the bubbling of a newly found rebellious streak, I decided to do it. How did I go about writing a real man? I had been writing about fantasies for so long I didn't know where to start.

I jumped to my feet, grabbed my purse, and left. "A-researching I shall go."

Since I'd been roped into writing about a fireman by my publisher, I headed to my local firehouse, notebook in hand and hope in my heart. But as I approached the actual building, my determination fizzed out, as if someone had poked a hole in the tire of my courage. By the time I arrived in front of the massive gray building, I was all out of air. I slumped into the low wall that ran just opposite the firehouse, shoulders hunched down and notepad in hand. Shit. I so didn't have the guts to go inside and start asking questions of the men in the yellow *hosen*. *I'm an introvert, for God's sake!* The longest conversations I'd ever had with a male stranger were in the checkout line at the supermarket.

"What are these called?"

"Parsnips," I replied with an all-knowing smile.

"Are they good? They look like dirty white carrots."

"They are very nutritious," I said, with full awareness of my vegetable geekiness.

With an artistic flip, I opened my notepad, pulled out the mermaid pen I snatched from my novelty pen collection, and started chewing on its plastic blue hair. I took on a pensive look I was hoping looked mildly attractive, while my brain went into overdrive. I could at least observe the great firemen from across the street and take notes. What did they do all day when there were no fires to put out? Was there any truth to the idea firemen always ate well and had a resident chef? Was there a spotted dog in every firehouse?

Two tall figures, dressed in funky-looking beige pants held up with bright red suspenders, came out into the driveway. My interest perked up and I straightened my back just enough not to look like my grandma. The tallest one had a basketball in his hands, and he bounced it off to the other guy. *Ah, a friendly game of basketball while they wait for the next great fire.*

I scribbled some notes and returned my attention to the two. I couldn't see their faces very well from across the street, but they seemed to be average-looking Joes, not the hot-to-trot firemen depicted in almost every romance ever published. Real men. The type I wanted to write about.

I should go talk to them. Maybe challenge them to a shoot-out. I remembered I was in heels and that I would rather poke out my eyes with a hot metal rod than address a male I'd never met with some random questions. I decided to stick to my notes instead.

I noticed them glancing at me every so often, but I couldn't see the expressions on their faces. *Are they wondering why there is a hot chick checking them out? Or maybe they are squabbling over which one should come and ask me out on a date.* Those thoughts were the reason I wrote about things I knew nothing about. Kind of like Jane Austen writing about relationships when she herself never seemed to have had one.

Whatever the guys were thinking, it was a moot point. They both rushed into the building, closing the door behind them, and left me salivating over the seed of a story beginning to grow in my head.

While I dug through my bag in search of that sweet-and-salty granola bar I knew I'd stuffed in my purse, someone else came out through the same side door. However, this time the fireman had no basketball in his hands, and he was crossing the street and walking straight toward me. A moment of panic sent my heart into a race against itself, and I felt my cheeks burn with such intensity I might very well need a hose to put out the fire. *What the f—?*

"May I help you with something?" The voice, pleasant and strong, was coming from a very tall fireman with the most intense green eyes I had ever seen.

4

Trick of the light? He was speaking to me, and my mouth had gone dry as a desert. Try as I may, I couldn't utter a single rational sound.

"Miss, do you need any help? You've been sitting there for the last hour, and the guys at the firehouse are wondering whether maybe you need some assistance."

Crap! I had been there for a whole hour already? Staring at the firehouse and those who dared come out for air once in a while?

"I'm no stalker." Of all the things I could have chosen to say, those words were probably not the right ones. Not if I wanted to make a good impression.

The fire dude laughed, a small dimple forming on his right cheek. He was cute. Not in an earthshaking, mind-blowing way, but very cute. His blondish-brownish hair stuck up in various spots as if he had run all his fingers through it. "We didn't say you were, miss. But you are making the guys a bit nervous. All that staring—"

I coughed to clear my throat. It didn't help. The words that always came so easy to me on paper didn't want to leave my lips. "Sorry. Didn't mean to freak you guys out." My shoulders hunched down as I deflated again. "I'm just a writer."

I may have whispered those last few words, but his head still snapped up with curiosity. "A writer? Are you writing about the firehouse?"

"Firemen." I had become monosyllabic, apparently. "Research."

The cute fireman wiped his hands on his pants and offered me one for a shake. "Hi, I'm Gavin McLeod." He took my hand in his and shook it enthusiastically. His hand was big and warm. I felt the calluses on his fingers against my soft palm. "You are?"

"Ana. Ana Mathews." Our hands were still together, moving up and down like a jump rope. *He is really cute.*

"It looks like a slow day today. Why don't you come inside and meet the guys?" *Oh, my God. Did he just invite me into the firehouse?* "We were just getting ready to have lunch. Care to join us?"

"Can I?" Okay, so that's two words. I seemed to have broken the monosyllabic spell. My hand was still cocooned inside his, and I wasn't going to lie; it felt good.

Gavin pulled gently on my hand, coaxing me from the wall. "Yes, of course. Come on. You can come and ask us whatever you want."

My butt felt weird, all numb from the cold cement wall, and I had the urge to wiggle it a bit. But I didn't. Instead I followed the tall, green-eyed man into the firehouse, my legs shaking like leaves in a summer breeze, and my palms, now freed from the warm shelter of his, sweaty and clammy.

I can do this. I can do this. Except I probably couldn't. My tongue had swelled to double its size—or so it felt—and my brain had been replaced by a wad of cotton balls as I crossed the threshold. Immediately I felt like a lamb who had just walked into a wolf-riddled meadow. Several pairs of suspicious eyes scanned me from head to toe, and this time even my overactive imagination couldn't turn those looks into what they were not.

"Hey, guys. Ana here is a writer and she is writing about a fireman." I had to give it to him; he was as enthusiastic about my nonexistent story as a little boy about a lollipop.

The other guys looked at me as if I had two heads at first, but then their faces opened in big welcoming smiles. Several almost stepped all over each other offering me a chair at the big rectangular table they were all sitting at. I picked the one closest to my green-eyed fireman and smiled nervously at the large group of men in the room. Why were there no women? I knew for a fact that there were several female firefighters in the neighborhood, but none of them were present that day.

The food looked basic but delicious. A mouthwatering scent of roasted meat and potatoes wafted up to my nose, making me swoon a little. I was pretty hungry. *Food myth? Check!* Losing my tendency for shyness and allowing my stomach to dictate my actions, I made a move toward the tray in the middle of the table to help myself to some meat and potatoes.

"Try the brussels sprouts." The guy across from me was smiling so big I thought he may tear the edges of his lips. "They are to die for." They were indeed.

"What kind of book are you writing?" That practically choked me. My mouthful of potatoes and sprouts made my cheeks look like those of a chipmunk storing food for the winter. I felt the heat climbing up my neck and burning through the skin of my face. What could I say without either offending them or making them laugh at me?

"Romance." I could barely hear myself, so I figured they couldn't either.

"Romance?" Okay, so I was wrong. The same guy from across the table had the ears of a freaking cat, apparently. "You're writing a romance about a fireman?"

I nodded, quickly trying to swallow the massive amount of food I still had in my mouth. "What? You're going to write one of us as this big sex god of a guy?" The men all laughed at his comment, and I couldn't find fault in it. They were a bunch of pretty plain-faced guys. Nothing too handsome or muscular about them. Real men.

With a big, noisy gulp, I finally swallowed the food. "No, that's the whole point. I want to write about a real guy, not a made-up godlike creature."

For the first time since we had sat down to eat, Gavin—who was admittedly rather handsome up close—turned to me and spoke. "But isn't that what romance readers want? Unrealistic beautiful guys with muscles to rival those of the Hulk?"

Aww, he was truly cute, and I caught myself staring

into his glittering eyes and imagining how it would feel to see myself reflected in them. "Well, yes. But some of us—me included—are getting a little tired of fantasy men."

"So what you're saying is that we're a bunch of ugly, puny guys that don't hold a candle to your usual romance heroes." The man with the cat ears was not done with me. I must have turned beet red, because he chuckled and slapped the table with a big hand. "Just teasing you, girl. Don't get your panties all in a bunch."

The mention of my panties in a room full of guys made me uncomfortable, but when Gavin gave me an apologetic shrug, I felt better. "I never said anything about ugly, just more… average."

The rest of the meal went without a hitch, and I found that I was having a good time. Where I'd earlier been in a panic, I was now relaxed and at home. I got email addresses from a few of them so I could use them as research sources, and the recipe for the roasted meat. I felt well-fed and content as Gavin walked me out into the driveway of the station.

"Thank you so much, Gavin. You guys were awesome." I held out my hand to him and was shocked when bolts of lightning ran through my arm as he took my hand within his.

"The pleasure was all mine—ours." A little smile popped on his lips. "Come and see us again."

Oh, I wanted that. I really wanted that….

***

Gavin

Try as I may, I couldn't get my mind off that quirky little number who had nearly electrocuted me with her touch. My whole body was alive with a fire that even the cold shower I took didn't temper. *Damn you, woman.* It wasn't her fault. Shit, she wasn't even that hot. A little curvier and shorter than what I normally went for, Ana was also much older than the girls I'd been seeing for the past few years. I hate sounding like a douchebag, but since my brush with death I decided to live it up—and living it up meant dating women who looked more like models and less like regular people. Not that I dated much. It was more of a collection of one-night stands, no strings attached. None whatsoever—not even the obligatory morning-after phone call.

When I first saw Ana, after the other guys joked about a female stalker outside the firehouse, I was not impressed. She stood just a couple inches over five feet, with dark brown hair haphazardly gathered into a bun, and unremarkable brown eyes. She did, however, have full lips that begged to be kissed.

Not sure where that came from.

But as the day went on, something strange happened; like a caterpillar, she suddenly turned into a butterfly. By the time she said goodbye, her hand stretched toward mine, I'd forgotten why I thought she was ordinary. Her messy bun suited her like a finely wrought crown on a fairy-tale princess, and her eyes, trained on mine, were like soft, delicious caramel.

Fireworks exploded as soon as our hands touched, and now, sitting on the edge of my bunk, all I could do was think about her luscious pink lips and how badly I wanted to savor them. *I've lost my fucking mind.* Something in my brain was finally coming unhinged after all these years. The doctors had warned me that there might be some long-lasting effects from the trauma I suffered in the accident. It was the only explanation.

"Are you coming or what?" Jason was standing at the door, holding on to the top of the frame as if it were a trapeze. "We're all waiting for you, idiot."

The guys were in the common room sitting around the small table, staring pointedly at the empty chair. I shook my head and sped up.

"The bionic man is here," I yelled as I made my entrance. They stared at me and chuckled. They had given me the nickname some time ago, and it stuck. "Get ready to lose all your money." I sat down and, swiping the three cards on the table in front of me, prepared for the usual downtime poker game.

***

Ana

"I love you. I truly, absolutely love you." I had promised myself not to open the package of Oreos my friend had given me the day before, but the little buggers were calling my name. I stood in the middle of the kitchen hugging the small package. They were the thin Oreos. *So they must also have less calories.* I sniffed the unopened box and felt my mouth watering. "Walk away, girl, walk away...."

In a swift move, I stuffed the box in my small pantry and ran upstairs. *Doing laundry will help get my head off the damned cookies.*

I was stuffing my undies in an already overstuffed washer when the strident sound pierced my ears. *Holy crap! What now?* Why was the fire alarm ringing?

"Shit! Dinner." In my recent Oreo adoration spell, I had forgotten I was cooking chicken for dinner. I was a legendary bad cook, but I had to eat. I sped down the stairs and was greeted by an alarming cloud of smoke. *My kitchen is on fire.*

I ran out the front door—but not before collecting my precious laptop from the office—and called 911. "My house is on fire." Well, at least I thought it was.

I waited on the lawn, laptop hugged tightly against my chest, my eyes never leaving my little house. Was I going to lose this awesome home I had bought from a distant cousin? I loved my home with its quaint white porch, curly snow guards on the black slanted roof, and the tiny screened porch off the kitchen where I spent a lot of my time writing. I had bought it for a song a couple years ago, taking advantage—I'm ashamed to admit—of my cousin's less-than-desirable financial predicament. Not that he had anyone to blame but himself, gambler that he was, but I still felt—however mildly—embarrassed every time I thought about it. And now my house, my pride and joy, was going to burn down to ashes all because of my cooking ineptitude. I made a mental note to take some cooking lessons in the near future, and looked up the road, searching for the fire truck I could hear in the distance.

The red truck, lights flashing, came around the curve and headed to my house. My heart was beating so loudly I could hear it over the shrieking of the sirens. I so hoped they got here in time to save my humble abode. As they parked the truck, several firemen jumped out of it, immediately immersing themselves into a frenzy of activity. Some were unrolling the hose while others held on to—were those axes? Oh, my God! Were they going to break through my vintage windows and doors? *If they have to, silly woman. Do you want the house to burn down?*

A short firefighter, covered from head to toe in the not-so-fashionable beige-orange uniform, strode toward me. As he approached, I realized *he* was a she. Her helmet hid most of her face, constantly sliding forward as she walked.

"Ma'am, where's the fire?" I looked at her stupidly, and then back at my house. Strange, I couldn't see any smoke anymore. "You said the kitchen, right? Is that in the back?"

I also couldn't smell anything burning, which was even stranger since I knew that smell all too well from all my past kitchen disasters. "Yes, the kitchen. There was a lot of smoke." Suddenly I felt I needed to justify their presence there, since it was becoming increasingly more obvious there was no fire at all.

She tried to scratch her head but couldn't slide her fingers under the helmet. "We just checked the kitchen in the back and there is some smoke but no fire. Are you sure?"

I wasn't sure of anything anymore. I clutched the laptop even tighter. "Well, I never saw flames but there was a lot of smoke... and the alarm was going off...." Hell, my cheeks were on fire. Maybe they could try to put *that* out. "Can you double check?"

"We can break in through the porch in the back...."

No, no way! I didn't want them ruining my screened porch. "I can unlock the door for you." She frowned, wrinkling her nose as if she had smelled a rat. "Or I can give you the keys." I handed her my house keys and watched as she waved a couple other firefighters to the front door.

The next few minutes seemed to stretch forever, waiting on the lawn for them to emerge from my burning house. By then I was beginning to doubt if there was even a small fire, much less one that would burn my house down. The uniformed firefighters came out and joined another one waiting outside. I couldn't help noticing how they were laughing and slapping each other on the back. Oh God! I was going to be the laughingstock of the neighborhood. There was no fire.

"Miss, all is well. We turned off the oven and aired out the kitchen." The voice of the approaching fireman was very familiar, caressing my ears with its warmth. "Just a case of overcooked chicken."

I could hear the amusement in his voice and prickled like a porcupine under attack. "I'm glad you find it amusing, but I couldn't tell. There was a lot of smoke."

The tall man stepped closer and removed his helmet, brushing his fingers over very messy dark hair. My heart stalled and I had to cough. This was the green-eyed guy from my research foray to the firehouse a week or so ago. Now I was truly embarrassed.

"Don't I know you?" His gorgeous eyes were scanning my face, his eyebrows knitted together.

I took a deep breath, feeling an urgent need to fan myself furiously, and dared myself to look him in the eye.

"Yes, Ana Mathews. The writer." If he didn't remember me I was going to have to set myself on fire. With all those firemen here, there was no chance I would actually burn too badly. "I ate with you guys at the firehouse the other day."

His face, well-defined cheeks and all, opened in a brilliant smile. "Of course, Ana the writer." Phew, he did remember me. "So glad to see you again, even if in... strange circumstances." He was too sweet.

What he meant was "an idiotic false alarm that brought all of us hardworking firemen to your house to put out a piece of charred chicken." I liked him. I really liked him.

"It seems I need some cooking lessons and some guidance on how to distinguish a real fire from a false alarm." I giggled a little, embarrassed that my second meeting with this man would be during a full-blown show of how much of an inept idiot I was.

Gavin waved a big hand in front of him. "It's a lot more common than you think." Was he being kind, or were there really a lot more idiots like me? "You'd be surprised how many times we get called and it ends up being nothing. Which is a good thing, by the way. A false alarm is way preferable to a real fire."

If he said so. I wasn't going to contradict him. I was too busy staring at his gorgeous emerald eyes. It was like staring into the depths of a forest and guessing the richness of life within. I made myself a mental note to write that line down for one of my novels, and smiled. "I have a lot to learn about firefighting." And then some.

He lowered his voice and bent toward me. "I could help you with some research. Maybe we could go out to dinner one of these days… or lunch." His smile took over his face and made the corners of his eyes crinkle. Not so average Joe after all. "As long as you're not cooking." His wink made me laugh.

"No chance of that happening." I would never in

a million years attempt cooking a meal for anyone else but me. "When?" Excited didn't begin to describe how I felt at the mere idea of having an intimate meal with this beautiful fireman. He may not be exactly the average man I was looking for, but I was very willing to explore the possibilities.

"What about this Friday? I'll be done with my shift, so I will be out by four. I can pick you up at six or seven." He licked his lips and my insides melted. I bet they tasted amazing. *Stop, dummy.* "After all, I know where you live now."

I giggled like a ninth grader who had been asked out by a senior to the Prom, and I may even have batted my lashes. "Six thirty?"

"It's a date." My heart did a little jig inside my chest. Someone called him from the truck and I noticed the lights were on again. "Uh-oh, gotta go. They've called us. See you Friday." He took off speeding toward the already moving firetruck, and leaped onto the running board. Before he climbed inside, he turned around briefly and waved at me.

Oh, shit! Was this really happening? All these years writing about handsome men falling in love with equally perfect women, and I was falling for someone who was a lot closer to the characters in my books than I ever would be. I was looking for a real man. A real man. Not a construct of imagination or wishful thinking. A man with a face that didn't come from the hands of a classic sculptor, with a body that had a bit of flab here and there, and didn't make a model look shabby by comparison. Gavin may not be muscled like Hulk or pretty like Legolas, but he sure didn't seem to have many physical flaws. I hadn't seen the rest of his body yet, true. The two times I'd seen him he had been inside those bulky, ugly overalls. For all I knew, he may have crooked legs and mismatched hips. *There is hope still.*

Who was I kidding? I wanted those legs to be perfect and the hips to be the narrow frame for a sexy butt. *I'm so screwed.*

Red Wine and Kisses

Gavin

The hot water flowed down my face, and my muscles immediately relaxed. I flattened my hands against the tiled wall, shifted my weight to lean against them, and allowed the shower to massage me, washing away the ashes and soot covering my skin. Even though the fire had not been anything major, the wind had sent the ashes spiraling over everything and everyone. From the corner of my half-closed eyes, I glimpsed the grayish water swirling like a tiny tornado into the drain by my foot.

Under the caress of the water, my mind wandered to one of the first calls of the day. It had been a strange case of mistaken fire-identity. I laughed under my breath, recalling Ana's face, flushed in embarrassment as she realized her kitchen fire was nothing but a piece of burnt chicken in the oven. I had the urge to cup her cheeks with my hands and kiss those tempting lips of hers. Instead I had asked her out on a date. What was I thinking? She was older, and almost certainly not interested in casual sex. I was on a mission to live my life to the fullest, and being tied down into a relationship was not part of the plan. We might as well be from different planets. Yet—

Fuck! My body responded to the memory of her ivory skin and full well-shaped lips, and I was hard as a rock in seconds. The curve of her generous breasts peeking from the unbuttoned top exploded in my mind as vividly as if she were standing in that shower with me. Of course, the thought of her under the running hot water next to my naked body just made things harder for me—so to speak. *I don't need this right now.* Only my body didn't seem to care. *It* wanted her.

In desperation, I turned the faucet to cold and screamed as the chilled water replaced the hot. That should do it, I hoped. A few minutes later, I hopped out of the shower and wrapped myself in one of the large white towels my mom had gifted the firehouse with. Why couldn't I take my mind off the little writer with the heavenly lips? Why was I this excited about a date with a woman I knew would want so much more than what I was willing to give?

The firehouse was quiet. Jackson was the only one up, standing watch for incoming calls while the rest of the squad slept. I slipped between the sheets of my bed after putting on a pair of thin joggers, and closed my eyes. Like a skilled thief in the dark, sleep evaded me, dreams of the brown-haired romance writer not affording me a moment's peace.

I swung my legs over the edge of the bed and tiptoed to the kitchen, where Jackson stood by the microwave heating up a cup of coffee.

"Hell, Jackson. Why don't you brew a fresh cup? Reheated coffee has to be the most disgusting thing in the world." I snatched another mug from the counter and headed to the coffee machine, limping a bit. My leg was sore tonight, obviously not too happy with the long stretch without a rest.

"What are you doing up, dude?" Jackson frowned at me. "You're going on almost fourteen hours without a rest." I had taken on a few extra hours for another fireman who had gotten sick.

I raked my hair with my fingers. "Can't sleep."

Jackson laughed. "A certain writer in your brain?"

Well, that was surprising. Was I that obvious? "What are you talking about? I'm just too hyped up to sleep."

"Bullshit." He snorted just as the microwave beeped. He took the hot mug from inside and blew on it. "You couldn't take your eyes off her this afternoon. You looked like my golden retriever staring at a T-bone."

Coffee pod in place, I pressed the brew button on the machine and inhaled deeply, the wonderful scent of freshly brewed coffee wafting up to my nostrils. I was very tired, dizzy even, but Ana wouldn't leave me alone.

"How old do you think she is?" I almost bit my tongue, but I trusted Jackson with my life. His opinion mattered to me.

"I have no clue. Thirtysomething, I'm guessing." He took a sip of the steaming liquid and wrinkled his nose. "This *is* disgusting."

I laughed and handed him a coffee pod. "Make a fresh one, idiot." Jackson waved my hand away. He was known for being thrifty and stubborn. "Come on, man. How can you drink that junk?"

"It's perfectly good junk," he said, taking another sip of the reheated coffee. "No use in wasting good coffee. And if you're wondering if she's too old for you, I'm pretty sure she's not. You guys are three, four years apart, tops."

My thirty-first birthday had come and gone a few months ago. I was far from a kid, but I was hell-bent on living like one. If my accident had taught me anything, it was to enjoy every minute of my life and waste no time or opportunities.

"We're going on a date." There, it was out. "Not sure it's a good idea."

Jackson frowned. "Why not? You're obviously hot for her, and she blushed every time you looked at her. Go for it."

"She's not that kind of girl."

"What kind? She's flesh and bone."

"Not the kind I normally go out with." The coffee slid down my throat, soothing the smoke irritation out of it.

"You have a kind?' Jackson laughed and poured the rest of his coffee in the sink.

I stood, favoring my good leg, mug in hand and thoughts flying out toward Ana again. How would her soft body feel wrapped around mine? I shivered, pleasure running like electricity through my veins. My friend stared at me, his eyes and mouth wide open.

"Fuck, you got it bad, man!" I wanted to protest, but he was right. I had it bad. "It's about time you find a good woman and settle your ass down."

My hackles came up, sharp and deadly. "Why do I need to settle down? Because of my disability? Is that what you guys think, that someone needs to take care of this cripple?"

Jackson raised his hands in appeasement. "Whoa, dude. No one's saying that at all. You're perfectly capable of taking care of yourself. I just meant it's nice to have someone steady in your life, someone you can trust and who's there for you when you need it. Like me and my wife."

I blew out a heavy breath, releasing the tension that had so suddenly bunched up in my chest. I was being a dick. "Sorry, Jacks. I was out of line. I know what you mean."

Fuck! Still sensitive about it even after all this time? Despite living a perfectly normal life, I still sometimes thought of myself as a cripple. Old scars healed slowly, apparently.

My friend and coworker took a step toward me and tapped me on the back several times. "It's all right. We all have our sensitive spots." He laughed. "Even me."

I glanced at him and smiled. "*You* have a sensitive spot? What would that be? The size of your head?" We all joked about his head, which was a weird, almost conical shape, but he always seemed to take it in stride.

"I'm proud of my cone head," he said, feigning outrage. "I'm not telling you what it is."

My eyes widened as an idea came to me. "Shit! Is it the size of your—?"

He raised a hand in front of my face to stop me. "Don't even say it! Or I'll punch the daylights out of you."

Laughter bubbled out of me in an unstoppable stream. "Oh my God! It is!" Jackson had turned beet red, and I may have been imagining it, but I could swear I saw smoke coming out of his ears. "Your secret's safe with me, dude."

I couldn't stop laughing, and eventually he joined in, his hands holding his stomach. The phone rang from the office and Jackson ran to answer it while I washed the two coffee mugs we had used, still chuckling under my breath.

The sound of the alarm rang through the house. Three pulses in a row. Well, there wasn't going to be any more sleep tonight. A three-alarm fire somewhere. Reluctantly, my exhausted body and I made our way to the ready room, where I quickly changed into my uniform and put memories of the alluring Ana somewhere on the back burner of my mind. Later. I would sort that issue later.

***

Ana

The dizziness was not getting any better. I continued to blow into the paper bag, but my anxiety attack just seemed to thrive on the challenge. "I can't do this. I can't do this." My litany of negative thoughts and words kept pouring out of my head and mouth like the effects of mental dysentery. I was having a hard time pulling myself together. Cute and tall Gavin would be at my door any minute to take me out on a date, and I was a mess of nerves and ill-disguised doubts.

The doorbell rang, and I almost jumped out of my skin. I had changed at least ten times, but for a moment I considered changing again. Smoothing out invisible wrinkles in my floral sundress—oh God, did I look a little too flowery and girly?—I slogged my way to the door as if my feet had grown attached to concrete shoes.

Not the fool I often appeared to be, I cautiously looked through the peephole and found the rather handsome face of fireboy Gav. Yes, I had already given him a nickname, a bad sign that meant I was getting a bit too attached to the idea of him. I swallowed the bile that had gathered in my mouth and unlocked the door.

The beige fireman pants—were they called overalls?—were not what I was expecting to see him wearing. Not exactly date gear. I suddenly felt overdressed. "Oh, I thought we were going—"

Gavin looked down at himself, spreading his arms and hands apart. "Sorry. I was on call and didn't have time to change." He looked up at me and gave me a blinding smile. Oh, boy! He was more than handsome. This guy was gorgeous. At least that's what my eyes were telling me. "If you don't mind, we'll stop at my place on the way to the restaurant so I can change."

Wait! Stop at *his* place? I was going to go inside this god's abode? And wait while he got undressed in the next room? My heart and other equally sensitive areas of my body were all aflutter.

"Sure. I don't mind."

He offered me his arm in an oddly old-fashioned but oh-so-charming way, and we walked together to his car, a pea-green Wrangler that looked way too high for my short legs to climb. I must have looked hesitant, because he swept me into his arms and gently set me down in the passenger seat. I was so surprised I wasn't sure I actually thanked him out loud.

"So, am I going to be in your next book?" He slipped into the driver seat with the ease and smoothness of a cat. "Are you going to give me one of these new beards and a tattoo?"

I laughed as he started the car and merged into the traffic. "What makes you think I would put you in my next book? And a beard?"

A stolen glance in my direction made my stomach somersault inside. "I may not read them, but I see the covers of all these romance novels. The guys are all big, muscled, tattooed, and with big beards." He was not totally wrong.

"Well, I want to write a real man as my hero." It slipped out before I realized I was going to say it. Heat flowed into my face and neck.

"Like Jackson? The guy that was sitting across from you?"

Now why would I write about someone else when I could be writing about Gavin with his gorgeous green eyes, thick lashes, and luscious lips? True, I hadn't quite seen the rest of him, always stuck inside those ugly, bulky clothes, but he didn't walk with a limp and he was strong enough to pick me up. Something told me the rest of him was as pleasant.

"Maybe." I was not going to tell him I couldn't get him off my mind and that I was sure my next hero was going to look a lot like him. "Do *you* have a tattoo?" I glanced at him from the corner of my eye and saw him smiling, his lips curving upwards on one side.

"Maybe." He was infuriating. Now I couldn't stop thinking of his maybe-tattoo and where it may be located. I crossed my arms in front of me and vowed not to talk again until we had arrived at his place. Which, it turned out, took only a few more minutes. He lived pretty close to my house. "We're here.

Need help dismounting?" *Nice. Teasing me now.*

"I'm fine." I wasn't. I was wearing a dress, and as I slid out of the seat, I nearly exposed my butt to the world. "Sometimes I hate being so short," I mumbled under my breath. The gallant firefighter had already reached my side and offered me his hand for support.

"I do have a tattoo." His whisper caressed my ear, his lips mere inches from it. I shivered, a frisson of pleasure beginning where his breath touched my skin and spreading like wildfire all over my body.

He lived in a condo above a small coffee shop, and as we climbed the stairs, the aromatic scent of roasted coffee wafted around us and made my mouth water. "How can you stand it? I would be craving coffee all day long."

Gavin walked in front of me, his boots clanking on the wooden steps. "I'm not here much. Between the firehouse and volunteering at the hospital, I don't have much time to smell the coffee." He laughed at his pun and stopped by a wooden door, taking out his keys.

"Make yourself comfortable while I go change." He pointed at his small living room and turned to walk away. Halfway down the hallway, he stopped and turned around. "You look beautiful, by the way." And he walked away, leaving me breathless and uncomfortably hot.

His living room was small but very comfortable, with a gray couch in front of a glass-topped coffee table and a couple of simple bookcases packed with books. Another small pile of books, a tray with a coffee cup, and a small picture album created a feeling of hominess.

He likes to read! He was getting less and less *real* now. A handsome guy who liked to read? I scanned the titles on the table and on the shelves, wondering whether his choice of literary works was less than savory, but I was blown over by the quality—and diversity—of his choices. There was a smattering of everything, from comic books to James Joyce. *Is that a romance I see?* Were these books a clever ploy to get bookish women like me to fall head over heels in love with him? If that was the case, it was working. Gavin may have never read a single title on his shelves, but I was smitten.

"Do you like to read?" Gavin was standing by the counter that separated the living room from the small kitchen, rubbing a white towel on his wet dark hair. He had changed into a pair of jeans and a white shirt that clung to his obviously well-built chest muscles and shoulders. I gasped. Damn! He was perfect! The top three buttons of his shirt were undone and revealed a light smattering of dark hair. I had never been very fond of hairy chests, but at that moment all I wanted was to run my fingers over it.

What is wrong with me?

I had lost my power of speech and couldn't think of a single thing to say. Nothing smart or interesting at least. "Yes, I love to read."

Gavin discarded his towel on the top of the counter

and ran his fingers through his hair, causing it to curl and spike everywhere. "I thought we would eat here. What do you think?" No thought came to mind other than *yes, yes, and holy shit, yes!* "I was planning on taking you to Joe's Bistro, one of my favorite places, but I thought maybe I'll just cook something quick and easy for us. Do you mind?"

Mind that a hot guy voluntarily cooked a meal for me? Was he serious? "Of course I don't mind. If you don't. I don't want to be too much trouble."

Gavin moved then and, for the first time, I noticed a certain oddness to his step. Nothing I could put my finger on. It was not a limp, but an unusual way of moving. Maybe he had crooked legs after all.

"No trouble at all. I enjoy cooking." The sun had landed smack in the middle of that living room as Gavin's lips stretched into a smile, and my body turned into a puddle.

I watched him as he busied himself in the kitchen, slicing onions, chopping carrots, and browning ground beef with the expertise of a chef and the sexiness of a dancer. "You're obviously not a rookie in the kitchen." The way he turned the contents of the frying pan with a simple flip of his hand was as hypnotizing as the pendulum on a clock. "Have you been doing this for long?"

"Since I was a kid. My mom was a chef at a trendy local restaurant and she used to take me with her when she couldn't get a babysitter—which was pretty often."

He stirred the contents of the pan, his eyes never leaving the now pinkish-brown meat. "I learned a lot from her and the other cooks. I also learned that cooking can be a whole lot of fun and super relaxing."

Should I ask? "Where was your father in all of this?" Damn, it came out before I could bite my tongue.

Gavin stole a brief glance at me before returning his attention to the chopped tomatoes he was transferring from the block to the pan. "He was never in the picture. When I was about two, he decided he was not too impressed with his family and decided to go get a new one." I flinched. Wow! That was cold. "He wanted my mom to be home cooking and cleaning for him. 'Why marry a chef if she's not going to cook for you every day?' So, he packed his bags and left us. A couple months later, he was engaged to another woman."

"What an asshole." I nibbled on a piece of baguette he had sliced and placed into a small basket. "Did he at least keep in touch?"

Gavin chuckled, wiping his hands on the towel attached to the waist of his pants. "Hell, no. I know I have a couple half siblings, but he never bothered to check on us and I could barely remember him. It's been me and my mom all this time." Bringing the wooden spoon to his lips, he took a taste. "Care to have a go?" He picked up another spoon, half filled it with the delicious-smelling mix of meat and vegetables, and with his other hand cupped underneath, offered me a taste.

His fingers, so close to my lips, made me shiver in delight. The food was yummy, but that was not what I had been craving all evening. *Behave, woman.* A simple taste and my mouth watered. "This is delicious. What is it?"

"Nothing fancy." He chuckled, dropping the spoon in the sink. "Shepherd's pie. My mom's favorite comfort food, and her own recipe." I watched as he mashed the potatoes and then layered them with the meat deliciousness. He slid the whole pan into the oven with a flourish and sighed with satisfaction. "Now, we have to wait a while. Glass of wine?"

Drinking was not my thing. In fact, I didn't like any kind of alcoholic drink, but I figured the occasion called for something different. Against my better judgment, I accepted a small glass of red wine, the only thing I could drink without gagging. We sat on the couch, side by side, with drinks in our hands. Our knees were nearly touching, a fact I was painfully aware of.

"Next you're going to tell me you like romantic comedies." If he said yes, I would throw in my hat. He laughed.

"Some are not too bad, but I do prefer something with a bit of mystery or action."

Phew, not so perfect. Good.

"You're not gay, are you?" I had to ask. I mean, he cooked, he read, he obviously kept his house nice and tidy... I had never met a man quite like that. Except in some of my books.

"I like women." Was I imagining it, or had his voice dropped an octave? "Why? Do I look gay?" His voice was back to normal, a lilt of amusement at the end of his question.

It was my turn to laugh. "I was wondering, because you just seem too perfect to be straight."

His eyebrows shot up. "I think I should take offense to that… for my whole gender, I mean. Are you telling me guys can't be perfect unless they have some feminine traits? In the name of all straight and gay guys, I must strongly protest." I laughed even harder at his look of outrage.

By the time we sat at the table to eat, my legs felt a little wobbly and my head swam. I had only drunk an inch of wine, but my body, unused to alcohol, was having a strong reaction to it. I needed to put something in my stomach. Fast.

The shepherd's pie was like ambrosia from the gods. I may have been a terrible cook, but I knew when I was eating good food. This was better than good. This simple comfort dish was worthy of a professional chef. My starving stomach was so grateful for the deliciousness of each forkful it was almost grunting in delight. I giggled, covering my full mouth with my hand. Man, I had a serious buzz on, the first one I had ever had. Probably not the best timing, considering whom I was with. For some reason, that thought made me giggle harder.

"Are you okay?" Aww, he was so sweet! He truly

looked concerned.

My eyes wandered to his lips, full and sexy, and I had an urgent need to kiss them. A wave of bubbly dizziness ran over my head again, and the next thing I knew I had jumped to my feet, dropped my napkin on the plate and, leaning over the small table, grasped a handful of Gavin's shirt, and kissed him full on the mouth.

***

Gavin

Honey and mint with a hint of rich red wine. Ana tasted like something out of a dream, and I couldn't get enough of her kiss. Even though she had barely touched it, the wine had obviously gone to her head too quickly. She hadn't hit me as the kind to grab a guy's shirt over dinner and devour him along with the shepherd's pie. Except that's exactly what she had done.

I wasn't complaining. At all.

With a moan of pure pleasure, I swiped my tongue along the inside of her lower lip, feeling the familiar flames of desire beginning to flare. My hands went around her shoulders to cup the back of her head and press her closer to me. Silently I cursed the table and the rest of the dinner still lying between us. Ana relaxed against my touch, and for a moment I thought she was going to fall flat on top of the dishes. I anchored her, and she whimpered.

"We should move to the couch, don't you think?" I was pretty sure she was far from thinking anything at that moment. Her eyes were closed and her arms flopped down along her sides, limp and powerless. She was drunk. "I'm not sure how you could have gotten drunk from a finger of wine, but you sure did."

Oblivious to my words, my sweet writer allowed me to support her and almost carry her to the couch. I didn't think her eyes ever opened. As much as I would have loved to continue the make-out session, I couldn't in good conscience. She was obviously unaware of what she was doing and probably wouldn't remember a thing the next day. Unlike me, who would forever remember exactly how she tasted and how she made my body burn and vibrate with a simple kiss.

I propped her on a couple cushions as her head lolled backward. Man, she was so intoxicated. I had never seen anyone get wasted on such a small amount of wine.

"Ana, can you hear me?" She whimpered again, and I yearned to squeeze her against me. "I'm going to make you some strong coffee and then I'll take you home, okay?" She mumbled something I couldn't understand, and I realized she would never last long enough for me to brew coffee. I had to take her home safely.

As soon as I walked away from the couch, she slid all the way down and almost fell off the edge, her head now buried between two cushions. I wondered where her keys were, and then I remembered her dropping them in her purse earlier. Her small purse was still sitting on the coffee table, but I hesitated. It seemed like a terrible breach of personal space to go through her things, but I needed to find her house keys if I was to take her home. It was either that or let her sleep at my place. I dismissed that idea quickly. There was no way I would be able to have her sleep so close to me.

"Come on, Ana. I'm taking you home." I tried to wake her up, but all I got from her was groaning. She was fast asleep. *Fuck. I have to carry her.*

Even though she was a tiny little thing, carrying an unconscious body was not an easy feat. I had done it a few times in my job, but adrenaline had been running high. This time, the only thing I was high on was the rush of hormones and blood to certain parts of my body. Not helpful at all.

"All right, girl. Let's do this." I slid one hand below her arms and another behind her knees and braced myself to pull her up. She was lightweight and soft even in her sleep. As I held her against my chest, Ana's head dropped on my shoulder, and her soft brown hair tickled my chin. An urge to kiss her took over me and I shook my head.

I'm such an idiot.

The drive to her house was quiet, the silence punctuated by her steady breathing and occasional whimper. I couldn't settle my pulse down, my blood still running fast and furious through my whole body. The mere proximity of her body was playing havoc with all my senses.

What is it about this woman that makes me feel this way?

I sighed deeply, half-relieved when we arrived at her place. I carried her inside and placed her onto the bed, dropping her keys on the nightstand. For a moment, I stood there, watching her sleep like an angel, flat on her back. The skirt on her floral dress had gathered beneath her and revealed a tantalizing portion of her milky thighs. The temptation to crawl on the bed and curl up against her was so strong my body shook like a leaf in the wind. I pulled the throw draped on the bottom of the bed over her sexy body and walked out of the room. I needed an icy-cold shower. Fast.

As much as I wanted to believe I was immune to her understated beauty, my body wouldn't allow me the illusion. I was very much taken by her petite frame, her thick brown hair, her soft honey eyes, and her luscious, sensual lips—pink kiss-me signs that pulled on me with the power of magnets.

Better get out of here fast.

I flew rather than walked out of her house, and drove home faster than ever before. Once I got there, I stripped off my clothes on my way to the bathroom and ran the water in the shower while I kicked off my shoes. Without hesitation, I threw myself under the running water, grateful for the shocking blast of cold that assailed my body. Just what I needed—or rather, just what I could have right then. What I truly needed was Ana. Her body glued to me, lips on mine, hands working whatever magic she had over my body and soul.

Damn! No shower is going to help me now.

Lobster and Fire

Ana

I was determined to stay locked in the house for the rest of…. Who was I kidding? Forever! I was never going to leave my house again. Inside my head, an eight-foot gorilla was pounding his enormous paws on my brain, and my limbs had turned into some kind of gelatinous material. I had never gotten drunk, so this was all new to me. Add the fact that I couldn't be more embarrassed for kissing my fireman over his delicious shepherd's pie, and I truly wanted nothing else than a chasm to open under my feet and swallow me whole.

Why, oh why had I thought that drinking was a good idea? Since my lips very rarely touched any kind of alcoholic substance, what made me think I could drink even the two fingers of red wine without feeling its effects tenfold? Now, not only was I as sick as a dog, but also totally and utterly mortified by what I had done.

It was a good kiss though. Gavin's lips had been soft and yielding when, fueled by the red devil, I inserted my tongue between them. His taste was heavenly—not that I had ever tasted anything heaven-bound. My body had liquefied and, if it hadn't been for Gavin holding me up, I would have fallen chest-first into the leftovers of our dinner.

The phone rang, loud and strident, and I moaned. Who could be calling me at—? I looked at the clock. Hell, it was already eleven and I was still in my pajamas. I slid my finger across the screen and gingerly placed the phone by my ear. "Ana speaking."

"Are you okay? I was worried about you." Oh, God! It was none other than sweet and hot Gavin. The last person I wanted to talk to right then. "You looked a little green when I dropped you off at your place last night." In fact, I didn't remember much of what happened after the infamous kiss. Not sure whether it was the wine or the fact I had blocked it out. I was so ashamed I had acted like a harlot. Shit, there it was again. The writer in me. Did anyone even use that word still?

"Hi, Gavin." I sounded like a penitent little girl who had just read her mom's spicy-hot romance novel. "I'm okay. A little hungover, that's all. Not too used to drinking, obviously."

Gavin's laughter came through loud and clear. He had a lovely laugh, bright and bubbly. "Yeah, I figured it. You only had an inch of wine. There was still some left in your glass."

I giggled and my head nearly exploded. "I made a fool of myself, didn't I?" Better come clean and call out the elephant in the room. "I'm sorry."

"Sorry for what? The kiss?" I knew I had kissed him—and loved every second of it—but hearing him say it out loud made my ears burn against the phone. "Why would you be sorry? I had been thinking about doing the same all evening." Wait! What? He *wanted* to kiss me? "You have by far the sexiest lips I've ever seen."

My friends would have to come and gather what was left of my body into a bottle. He thought I had sexy lips. Was he teasing me?

"Really?" I was not very good at repartee.

"Yes, really." His laughter had stopped and his voice was low and warm, seeping through the phone speaker like a love song. "It was a great kiss. Even though I'm not sure you were 100 percent aware of what you were doing." I laughed nervously. "I would like to go out with you again, if that's okay. I'll even help you with the research for your book. I can be the *real guy* you're looking for." Oh, no, he couldn't. He may not be a Hulk-type guy and have his body covered in tattoos, or have a face that rivaled Dorian Gray's, but he surely wasn't ordinary.

I cleared my throat. "I'd like that." I couldn't get over the fact he thought my forever-dry lips were sexy. Not cute or sweet. S-E-X-Y.

"I'm off this Saturday. Picnic by the lake?"

This was the best thing that had happened to me since the day I got my first book contract. I had been divorced now for longer than I had been married, and I had to admit that, even though I wrote romances for a living, I had pretty much given up on love. While many of my friends began looking for the companionship of men shortly after their divorces, I ran the opposite way. My life experiences with romance were so far from ideal they might as well be from different planets. But at that moment, as Gavin asked me out, a little flame of hope and excitement lit up in my heart.

I wasn't sure it was a good thing.

By the time I hung up, my heart was racing in my chest and my fingers were itching to write. Unfortunately, my hangover was less than cooperative, my head still pounding with every movement, every flash of light. So, I took a nap instead.

When I woke up a couple hours later, I felt even worse. I knew better than thinking naps would refresh me. Ever since I was a child, any naps I took, no matter how brief, always made me feel worse. My mom used to say my wires must be crossed, since I was the only kid in kindergarten that woke up grumpier than before her nap. My head was not hurting like before, but now I felt as if I was sleepwalking. *Maybe I am.*

"Delta, can you come over?" Delta was my best friend. Unlike me, she was an extrovert that lived to socialize. The little social life I had I owed to her always trying to drag me to events. In the terribly bleak days after my divorce, Delta had been my rock. My mother lived on the other side of the country at the time, and even though she was always willing to talk and listen to me, it was not the same thing as having a shoulder to cry on. A real, flesh and bone one. Delta was it.

"What happened?" From the other end of the line, her voice sounded concerned. "Are you okay?"

I yawned, and a flash of pain shot through my temples at the movement. "I'm fine. A little hungover." I heard her intake a big gulp of air. "Yes, Delta, I drank last night. And yes, I'm probably out of my freaking mind."

"Was it at a party?" Come on! She knew me better than that.

"No, I was on a date." She didn't let me finish. I had to pull the cell phone away from my ear, afraid that all the squealing coming from the other end would make my head explode. "Don't get too excited. It was sort of a—" Hell, what was it exactly? "Research date, I guess."

Delta laughed. "How scientific of you. Does it involve experiments, or is it purely theoretical?"

I had to giggle. She always made me laugh. "Stop making fun of me. Research for a book. My publisher wants me to write a novella about a fireman, and he's one."

I could hear the clucking of a tongue and I could imagine her face clearly, her eyes squinting in playful suspicion, her head shaking from side to side in mock disapproval. "Oh, he is, is he? Has he started a fire or is he putting it out? Or both?"

My first instinct was to deny it, but the truth was he was indeed starting a fire in my heart and other parts of body. One I hadn't felt in a very long time and had given up on. "He's very cute." The understatement of the year. He was so hot my eyes were scorched every time I looked at him.

"Give me twenty minutes to put on some makeup and I'll be right over." Delta didn't wait for goodbyes, and I was left listening to the dead signal.

I might as well take a quick shower and down a couple cups of coffee if I was going to be semifunctional for the rest of the day. As I collected a fresh towel from the linen closet, my laptop caught my eye. Oh, shit. It was calling me again. The ideas and feelings in my brain and my heart were exploding like popcorn in a hot pan, and my fingers were literally itching to write them down. I resisted. I really did. But after a few moments of standing there, holding the soft towel against my chest, the laptop and my muse won. All thoughts of a warm shower shoved aside, I sat in front of the devilish contraption and began typing away.

When the bell rang, I snapped out of my semihypnotic state and groaned. *Man, I stink*. Delta wrinkled her nose when she laid eyes on my disheveled hair and smeared mascara.

"Wow! You got it bad." I stared longingly at my

computer, half regretting having called her. "Don't even think about it, woman. You're not going to write. You're in urgent need of a shower." She laid her hands on my shoulders and pushed me toward the bathroom. "I'll brew some coffee while you wash up."

The hot water falling over my face and shoulders felt heavenly. For a while, I forgot the soap and stood still, allowing the relaxing spray to hit me straight on the face and run freely down the rest of me. My muscles relaxed and my mind stopped racing. Delta called out my name from outside the door, waking me up from my wet reverie. Wearing only a towel and with my hair dripping, I opened the bathroom door and strolled to the living room, from where the tantalizing scent of fresh-brewed coffee emanated.

"Shit, Delta. That coffee smells—" It felt as if I'd hit a wall. Right in the middle of my messy living room and wearing an expression I couldn't decipher—was it delight? Surprise maybe?—was my current inspiration for a not-so-common firefighter. I nearly choked on my own tongue. "Gavin? What—?"

His grass-green eyes scanned me from top to bottom and his jaw dropped. I belatedly remembered I was half naked, and grabbing a pillow from the nearby couch, attempted to cover myself. To no avail. The stupid pillow was the size of a wash rag and totally useless in terms of a buffer between my wet, too-exposed body and his hungry eyes.

"Sorry, I thought you knew I was here." Like a

gentleman, he finally averted his eyes, but he had already had an eyeful. Fuming, I glanced at my best friend who stood next to him, arms crossed and a conniving little smile on her lips. She did it on purpose. She knew all too well that I'd be coming out of that bathroom in a very immodest state of seminakedness and did nothing to warn me. *I'm going to kill you.* My telepathic abilities seemed to be off, because she smiled even bigger.

Without another word, I fled from the room to go slip into some yoga pants and a T-shirt. How mortifying— and yet rather exciting—to be caught in that state by the one man I was—*do I dare think it?*—falling for. Upon my return to the room, my cheeks blazing and my heart flipping around like an acrobat on crack, Gavin stopped talking to my traitor friend to focus solely on me. I liked that. A lot.

"I'm so sorry, Ana. I had no idea—" Looking appropriately contrite, Gavin searched for words without much success. I was a writer and I was having trouble finding them myself.

"I've a feeling neither you nor I had much to do with this." I threw a pointed stare at Delta, who was now sitting on the armchair, her legs crossed demurely and an innocent smile on her face. *Stop it, Delta. I know exactly what you're up to.* "Why did you come over? We just talked on the phone."

"I forgot to tell you, you left something at my house last night." Delta blinked briefly, and I watched as she licked her lips like a wolf slobbering over a fat lamb. Gavin stretched his hand to me. "I figured you'd need this."

It was my writer's notebook, the little pink pad I carried around with me in case ideas just came knocking out of the blue. A good writer could never be taken by surprise, and muses were finicky beings.

"Thank you for bringing it over." Our fingers touched as I retrieved the notebook from his hands, and I swear I felt as if a bolt of lightning had come down from the skies and baked me from the inside out. "Coffee?"

Delta was still giving me that funny look of hers that spoke louder than words. *"He's hot,"* it said. *"I will date him if you don't."*

Think again, my friend.

Before she could stand up and go get Gavin the coffee, I did it myself, quickly returning with a steaming mug of dark roast and sitting next to him on the couch. I didn't do it on purpose, but somehow our knees ended up touching each other, causing a pleasant kind of burning to go up my leg into my thigh and beyond.

"I know we had set up a date—" He lowered his voice and looked sideways at Delta who—nosy as she was—was tilting her head so she could better hear what he was saying. "But I wanted to see you sooner. The notebook was a terrible excuse." He chuckled softly, sweeping a hand over his luscious lips.

If the smile on my face was as wide as the one I felt inside of me, I must have looked like a total fool. "I'm glad you came, even though I do wish I was dressed more appropriately—or at all." We both laughed, the memory of his eyes on my half-naked body making me flush all over again.

"Were you always a fireman?" It was Delta, who could not keep quiet for more than a few minutes at a time. My angry glare didn't make a dent in her resolve to fish for more information. "How old are you anyway? Twenty-six? Twenty-seven?"

Gavin smiled. "More like thirty-one. No spring chicken here." He looked at me as if apologizing for not being in his twenties anymore. I smiled even wider. I was thirty-four and very glad to find out he was in my age group. "I've been a fireman for a long time, even though I did have other odd jobs beforehand."

"Does it pay well?"

I was flabbergasted. How dare she? That was way too personal of a question. I loved Delta, but she had no filter whatsoever.

In his defense, he took it in stride. With a soft chuckle, he shook his head. "God, no. The pay is awful. The only reason I can live off it is because my father left me a small fortune when he died some years ago."

I was horrified that he sounded so blasé about his father's passing. "I'm sorry to hear about your father."

"I know I sound kind of stonehearted, but I didn't know my father well at all." He must have noticed the shock on my face. "I told you that he left my mom and me when I was only two years old, never to come back. I guess he felt guilty about it, and a few months before his death he contacted me to tell me he had named me in his will as an heir to most of his considerable fortune."

Delta was leaning forward, obviously enraptured by the story. Man, did she love drama!

"At the time, I didn't think much of it. I wanted nothing to do with the man who had left us with nothing." Gavin's voice had gone flat, and his beautiful, vibrant eyes dulled. "But less than a year after, we were notified that he had passed away and had left me quite a bit of money. Apparently, he died of colon cancer."

Half-consciously I scooted closer to him, my hand automatically seeking his. "Oh my God, I'm so sorry." Gavin accepted my small gesture of comfort and entwined his fingers with mine. "And he never actually talked to you?"

His eyes hardened. "He tried, but I never gave him the chance. I was too angry with him. Where was he when I needed a father and my mother was struggling to make ends meet? I'm not sure I've forgiven him even now."

Delta leaned farther, her eyes shining with interest. "How long ago was this?"

None of your business, girl. But I wanted to know, if truth be told.

"Hell, more than seven years ago now." His eyes

came alive again. "It was right after my accident."

As if we were on the same exact wavelength, Delta and I exclaimed at the same time, "What accident?"

He laughed and my heart melted even further. He was so sweet. "I had a big car accident about eight years ago. I was in the newspaper and everything." He chuckled again and licked his lips. "Not the best way to get famous, I guess."

"Well, you obviously survived." Delta, the no-filter queen. "Were you seriously hurt?"

I threw her another warning glare, but to no avail.

"I was in the hospital for months. I think the news was what made him contact us." He was silent for a moment, as if digesting what he had just said. "Funny how tragedy makes everyone reevaluate their lives."

Taking advantage of his hand in mine, I gave it a little squeeze, delighting in the warmth of his skin against mine. "I'm glad you're okay now."

His gorgeous eyes locked with mine. "I've never been as happy to be alive as since I met you."

Good thing I was sitting down. My legs turned to Jell-O and my heart began beating so fast I was afraid I would have a heart attack. We stared into each other's eyes, momentarily forgetting the presence of my friend in the room. Until she not-so-delicately coughed out, "Cheesy."

If my eyes could shoot actual bullets, she would have been a colander right then.

As if waking up from a dream, Gavin let go of my

hand—I may have sighed at that point—and got to his feet. "I'm so sorry. You guys were having a girls' day and I barged in on you without warning. I better go."

I wanted to protest but thought better of it. The last thing I wanted was to seem needy.

"See you soon?" I had followed him to the front door, where he turned around suddenly and I almost crashed into him. My hands went to his chest and a tiny sound of admiration for such strong pecs escaped my lips. "Sorry."

Gavin looked behind me and then, lowering his face, he brushed his lips across mine in a brief but maddening caress. "Can't wait." He opened the door and was gone, leaving me with this feeling of emptiness. Shit. I was head over heels already.

***

Gavin

The tones woke me up from a rather erotic dream and a giant, deep groan left my lips even before my eyes popped open. *Shit!* The last thing I wanted to do after dreaming of Ana's delicious—and very naked—body was to rush to go fight a fire. I was fighting a blaze of my own—one that wouldn't be quenched with water.

I dragged myself out of bed, adjusted my overstimulated body parts inside my clothes, and quickly slipped the hanging elastic suspenders over my shoulders, and my arms into the sleeves of the tunic. My helmet lay on the small dresser by my bed and I grabbed it on the way out the door. Jackson's voice came on the loudspeaker telling us it was a structure fire not too far from where we were and that there seemed to be several people still stuck in the house.

After all the years of practice, it was now easier to jump into the cabin of the fire truck propelled solely by my arms and one leg. As I tied the air tank to my back, I turned on the ignition, the sirens, and the lights, and we were on the move. Jackson, sitting next to me, buckled on his breathing gear as well and adjusted his helmet as he proceeded to give us more information about the incident through our helmet intercoms.

The air was thick with smoke as soon as we turned the corner of the street. People were standing on the sidewalks, many in their nightclothes, a mix of curiosity and horror stamped on their faces. My colleagues jumped out of the truck even before I had it totally stopped. I jumped after them and immediately engaged the pump and began to stretch the line. Jackson was already inspecting the structure, and the other men were coming back toward me to get their lines.

As usual, the squad worked in perfect synchrony, like a well-oiled machine. My job was to make sure my men had what they needed when they needed, often having to anticipate it. After the accident, I'd thought my days as part of the unit were done. When Jackson had offered me the engineer's gig, I didn't hesitate. It wasn't the same as before, but I'd still be doing what I loved and with the people I considered my second family. Sometimes I wished I could do more, but most of the time I was happy to be the support for these great guys. After all, what kid had not dreamed of driving a fire engine?

By the time we got back to the station, dirty and exhausted, morning was peeking through the thick clouds. Work was not done though. Until all the equipment, including the truck, was clean, inspected, and ready to go again if necessary, no one in the station was resting. By the time everything was done, my shift was over and I could go home.

After a quick shower, I literally fell face-first onto my bed and fell asleep. Normally I didn't dream after a night's work, but that day I had vivid dreams. Pleasant dreams that involved a certain tiny writer and her ability to make me come undone with a smile.

***

Ana

I remember being a young girl and thinking that time passed by with the speed of a very tired slug. As I got older, it was almost as if the slug got exposed to some weird radioactive rays and became Super-Slug, flying by at the speed of light. However, it seemed as if my childhood unfriendly slug had returned to plague my days, for the week couldn't have gone by any slower. I couldn't wait for Saturday and the promised picnic with Mr. Fireman, and yet the hours, minutes, even tiny seconds ticked away so slowly I had to wonder whether time itself was running out of batteries.

I had changed clothes at least ten times, and came to the realization that my wardrobe was not date-friendly at all. Saturday was finally here, and there wasn't a single piece of clothing in my closet that I considered worthy of such a momentous occasion. *I may have to go shopping.* There was no time though. Gavin would be here in less than an hour, and I was still in my underwear with a rat's nest for hair and a face covered in red splotches. Out of desperation, I finally picked a pair of jeans and a plain black T-shirt with a nice, ocean-blue scarf for a splash of color. I slipped on my comfortable Skechers and focused on making my hair halfway presentable.

The last couple days had been hectic. I was a bundle of nerves thinking about what may—or may not—happen during this much-dreamed-of date with Gavin. He was obviously interested or he wouldn't have kissed me. Well, okay, the first time I had been the one doing the kissing, but he had admitted to liking it. That was good news, right? I hadn't dated in so many years I had no idea what was a good sign.

My marriage had been far from a success—more like a succession of battles and failed attempts at preventing something that had never been meant to work from failing. Even though I didn't believe in fate, my marriage had been doomed from the get-go. My ex-husband and I had nothing in common. And when I said *nothing,* I totally meant it. I was an introvert; he's an extreme extrovert. My idea of a fun night out involved a dark movie theater and ridiculous amounts of buttered popcorn. His was a crowded floor at a hard rock concert involving absurd amounts of beer. I was a solid believer in abstinence from drugs—I made an exception for coffee and chocolate—but my ex was a true follower of the mantra "the higher the better." I was a dog person; he liked cats. I watched sci-fi and rom-coms; he loved watching the Transporter beating guys into a pulp for 95 percent of the movie. We just couldn't agree on the simplest of things, and we fought like a cat and dog from the first day we met until the day we went our separate ways. I didn't hold a grudge against him, even though he'd broken my heart. It was both our faults to think we could ever work as a couple. But after that experience with a relationship, I had written out love for good. Or I'd thought I had.

A brief glance at the bathroom mirror told me I had achieved the closest I was ever going to get to perfection. My makeup was in place, with no red blotches in sight, the outfit was simple but sexy-ish, and my hair had been successfully tamed into a bun. I was ready.

Except I wasn't. As soon as the bell rang, my stomach rumbled and I had to rush to the bathroom with the heaves while perfect Gavin waited outside my door.

"Are you okay?" Gavin's brow wrinkled in worry. It had taken me a good five minutes or more to open the door, and I may have looked a little harassed.

"Sorry, I was in the room and didn't hear the bell ring." I hoped I still looked half presentable, because he looked amazing. My throat went dry and I could almost see my eyes bulging like Daffy Duck's in panic. Not a good look. "You look good." *Did I say that out loud?*

Gavin chuckled, his sexy lips curling up in the corner. "You don't look too bad yourself. Are you ready to go?" He offered me his hand, and I didn't think twice before taking it in mine. It was warm and soft, big enough to fully envelop mine.

The drive to the park was a blur. I was so aware of his body next to me I couldn't focus on anything else. Was this what happened when you hadn't had sex in so long? Or was I just starved for the pure, unadulterated romance I wrote about? *It's a fantasy, woman. Only a fantasy.* But the beautiful man next to me defied every "rule" I had set for myself through the years in terms of relationships and the expectations that came with them.

The Jeep stopped abruptly—or it just felt that way to me—at an empty parking lot by Princess Anne Park. I giggled, wondering whether he had picked this park on purpose because of its name. The glint of amusement in his eyes confirmed my suspicions. *Well played, Gavin.*

"I thought you deserved to enjoy a park named after your namesake." I had not been named after Princess Anne, or any princess for that matter. My mother, ever so practical, had picked the first name she heard mentioned in the hospital after my birth. Thus, I was named for some stranger who just happened to be wandering the hallways of the maternity ward that fateful day.

I was not going to bust his romantic bubble.

After helping me slide ungracefully out of the car, Gavin walked a few steps ahead of me, periodically looking back as if making sure I was still following him down the steep, beaten-dirt path. Picnic basket in hand, he walked in that slightly unusual way I had noticed before, not quite a limp but a bit awkward and stiff. It was more noticeable now that he was navigating a path made slippery by the loose dirt and pebbles along the downward walkway. I wondered if it was a leftover effect from the accident he had mentioned the other day. Not that it damaged his cool, handsome demeanor in the least. In fact, it made him look sexier in my book. Then again, the man could probably puke in front of me and I would think it hot.

Once at the bottom of the hill, Gavin led us to a clearing among the thick cover of the trees and spread the blanket he had draped over his shoulder on the ground. With a flourish, he motioned for us to sit on top of the bright-colored covering and then set down the basket.

"Hopefully to your liking, princess." Gavin squinted and grinned as I pretended to study the blanket, my lips pursed and my hand flat on my face. "Well?"

"It could be a little more grandiose." My final verdict was met with a gasp of mock outrage. "I mean, it wouldn't hurt if it had a gilded throne, stuffed with downy cushions and all, but I guess it will have to do."

Gavin waited for me to make myself comfortable on the spread before lowering himself to the ground as well. I noticed that odd stiffness in one leg, as if it was painful for him to bend it suddenly.

"Does it hurt?" I had obviously been away from human contact for far too long. What in heaven's name possessed me to say that? What if it was something he preferred not to talk about, or brought bad memories? *You're becoming an idiot, woman.* But instead of looking confused or upset about the uncouth question, he looked pointedly at his legs, an eyebrow raised into a deep arch. I nodded.

"Only when it rains." He laughed at his joke and shook his right leg as if to prove it didn't bother him. "Side effects from my car accident. It does not hurt at all, just doesn't bend as quickly as I would like."

Gavin had scooted over to sit beside me, his long legs stretched in front of him as he leaned back on his arms. My glance skittered over to his magnificent biceps, bulging from under the short sleeves of his white T-shirt. They were perfect, not too built up, not puny. Just the right balance between grace and strength. So much more my type than the guys I always wrote about. Maybe Gavin could be my "real man" after all. Inspired by that thought, I studied him closely from under half-closed eyelids. My hero—because in my imagination, he was indeed a hero—was not pretty, with his nicely proportioned face, straight nose, emerald-green eyes, and the sexiest lips I had ever seen. For all sense of purpose, he was handsome but not unrealistically so. All in all, he looked like a somewhat average guy.

Oh my God! He *was* my real man!

"If you don't close your mouth, you're going to end up eating a fly." I realized with a start that I had been staring at him, agape and starry-eyed. He scooted closer, his left thigh now touching mine and sending tiny frissons of pleasure running through me. "Or I could just close it for you." My heart jumped in excitement as his voice became a thick whisper. With a subtle twist of his upper body, he leaned toward me. "A totally altruistic action, of course."

For once, I didn't want any more talk. I leaned toward him and met him halfway, our lips melding and latching on as if we were both starved for each other. In my romance novels, I always described the guys' taste as musky and spicy. Gavin's was none of that. He tasted of sunshine and rain, chocolate and wine, winter days by the fireplace and summers on the sand. My fireman tasted of life and joy. His kiss filled me with an energy

I hadn't felt in years. Was that what hope felt like?

"Much better than a fly." Had I said that out loud? I must have, because Gavin chuckled quietly against my lips, our foreheads and noses still touching. His hand was resting on my shoulder, its warmth burning pleasantly through the thin cotton of my T-shirt. I yearned to touch him, but we had known each other for a fairly short time and my romantic track record was far from stellar. *Slowly, girl, take it slowly.*

"Maybe we should put something else in our mouths for now." I opened my eyes wide and gasped at my own words. Gavin laughed. "I mean, food. We should put some food in our mouths."

Still chuckling, he bent forward to open the picnic basket. "I didn't take you for a dirty mind, Ms. Mathews."

My cheeks burned in embarrassment, but I laughed along as he took a plastic container and two glasses from the basket. "What do you got there, chef?"

He smiled at me and handed me the container. "Cucumber and watercress sandwiches—I'm watching my waistline." He chuckled again. "And lobster rolls."

My mouth dropped open. I absolutely loved lobster. "That's my favorite." He winked as if he already knew that. "How did you guess?"

"You mentioned it during our firehouse lunch." I remembered now. One of the guys had mentioned his love for everything seafood and I told them I had fallen in love with the lobster rolls I had while on vacation in Maine. "We have to put them together, but it's pretty simple: open the rolls and fill with the lobster meat. You said you like them simple, with no mayo or celery."

"Just the cooked meat." I was touched he remembered that. My ex-husband couldn't even tell what my favorite food was, much less how I liked it prepared. It was rather impressive—and sweet—that Gavin had picked up on that.

We got busy with the food. Gavin poured us some fresh lemonade—"I remember the last time you had wine"—and we sat for hours, talking and laughing the day away. It was strange how easy it was to be with him. I felt no pressure to do anything or be any particular way. I was able to be my quirky, awkward self without fear of being harshly judged by the handsome man beside me. I was having so much fun time ticked away too fast, and the next thing I knew, it was time to go home.

"We'll have to do this again soon." Gavin had packed all the dishes and leftovers in the basket, and helped me fold the blanket. "I had a lot of fun."

When we folded the blanket one last time, our bodies came close together, as if a magnetic force pulled them in. I looked up at his eyes and lost my voice. We stood there, staring in each other's eyes, hands barely touching as we held the spread, in silence. I could hear my heart beating furiously. Or was that his heart?

"I want to kiss you again," he finally said softly.

"Can I?"

I nodded, incapable of uttering a word as he bent down. Good thing we weren't home, because I was almost certain I would have pulled on his clothes until they came off. It was too soon for that. I wasn't ready. His lips lingered on mine, gentle and patient, as if we had all the time in the world. I was the one whose body and heart burned with urgent desire. Shit, I wanted this man.

"The firehouse is having a friendly basketball game against the fifth precinct." Our lips had parted, and yet I could still taste them. "Do you want to come? Where there are firemen and policemen, there is always lots of food and material for your romances." Oh my God! He even understood my writer's mind. "Will you come?"

Of course I would go. A million times over. I would go to the ends of the earth if he asked me.

Gavin smiled and kissed me again. That's when I saw the supernova.

Soup and Basketball

Gavin

The hoses were folded and in place, the equipment cleaned and ready, and the engine sparkled in the sunlight. I threw the dirty, wet rag in the bucket and clapped my hands once.

"Is that your new thing?" Jackson had appeared out of nowhere—or so it seemed. He had an amused smile on his lips and a mischievous twinkle in his eye. "Applauding yourself for work well done?"

For a moment, I wished I still had the rag in my hands so I could throw it at him. "Shut up, idiot. I was just getting rid of dirt."

"Go get cleaned up. I'll move the truck inside." I threw the keys to him and picked up my bag from the floor where I had dropped it once I decided the truck needed a bit of fixing up before the game. "We don't want your girl to be repelled by your messiness."

Jackson had seen Ana and me outside kissing a bit earlier, and was acting like an old yenta, nosy and hell-bent on pushing us together.

"She's not my girl." *Yet, anyway.* But I wanted her to be. More than anything I ever wanted in life. Shock didn't even begin to describe how I felt faced with such a revelation. We had gone out a few times since our picnic. Nothing too earth-shaking and yet, here I was actually contemplating a real and lasting relationship, two short months after we'd met. "I do need a shower though. Make sure not to crash the engine into the wall while you back it up."

I was being purely facetious. Jackson was our lieutenant and fully versed on how to operate and park a fire engine. With a wave, I darted inside the building to get ready. After hours of work under the sun, I smelled rather ripe. The shower called, and I obeyed.

Sometime later, cleaned and refreshed, I slipped into my shorts and sneakers, ready to take on the world. I couldn't wait to see Ana again. Even though I had been with her outside not even an hour ago, I was itching to feast my eyes on her gorgeous face and taste her lips again. God, I was in so deep I would never be able to dig myself out.

"Hey, Gavin. Give me a hand here, will you?" It was Derik, struggling with a giant pan in the kitchen. I detoured toward him, laughing.

"What the hell are you doing, man?" Derik, a tall, skinny man with a mop of black curly hair, held on to the pan's handles for dear life.

"Trying to pour some of this soup into the storage containers, but the fucking pan is heavy and awkward." I reached out to take over one of the handles while he tipped the pan over just enough to pour some of the thick liquid out. "I've been calling those idiots outside, but no one is paying attention."

The pan was heavy, and so big it was hard to keep it balanced as we tilted it farther and filled several plastic containers with its contents. "Couldn't you have waited until after the game to do this?"

The usual cacophony of raised voices reached us from outside the building. The men were getting ready to start the game, and probably waiting for me.

"Dude, let's hurry. They're waiting." What I didn't say was that I was more worried about making my writer wait than my buddies. My stomach clenched in anticipation of her eyes on mine. Shit. I had either struck lucky or out completely. Not sure which yet.

Pan finally emptied, and with the containers covered and placed safely in the fridge, I rushed to the door, half running, half hopping. My heart tap-danced all the way, and almost exploded when I opened the door and laid eyes on my beautiful Ana. She was sitting on the low wall across the way, her eyes searching for something—hopefully me.

The guys teased me for having taken so long inside and I gave them the finger, my eyes on Ana all along. I raised my hand and waved until she looked my way.

65

Even across the distance, I saw her eyes open wide and her face blanch. *What the hell is happening?* I followed her eyes down to my legs and it hit me. She didn't know. Fuck. She didn't know.

The game was a blur. I bounced, dribbled, stole the ball from my opponents, and shot it at the basket without much conviction or success. My head was not on the game. It was stuck on the look of surprise—or was it horror—on Ana's face when she saw me in shorts for the first time. I hadn't even considered that she may not be aware of my disability. Now what? How was she going to react? Was she going to accept it and move on, or be repulsed by it and run?

I should have told her. Too late now. I had assumed she knew, and now I had to be ready for whatever her reaction would be. *Calm down, idiot. She's not that shallow.* At least I hoped she wasn't.

As soon as the game was over—I think we won, but am not sure—I high-fived the other guys out of habit and sped toward Ana. She was still standing by the low wall, looking slightly confused and dazed. This was it. I crossed my fingers, swallowed hard, and got ready for… what, I could not guess. I was ready.

Or maybe not.

***

Ana

Delta had spent a whole evening planning my outfit, a slutty combination of a skintight dress and net stockings. I wouldn't be caught dead wearing it to a club, much less to a friendly basketball game between the firemen and the cops. I would be arrested for indecent exposure, most likely. However, I knew my friend and arguing with her was a waste of everyone's time. So, I humored her, nodding throughout the whole affair, and as soon as she left I threw the horrible outfit into the charity pile I had been collecting in my bathroom. I was not going to look like Julia Roberts in one of the earlier scenes of *Pretty Woman* just to please my insane friend.

This morning I had calmly picked up a pair of jeans and an Austen quote T-shirt, got dressed, and then spent the next hour trying to decide which shoes to wear. After trying on every pair of footwear I had in my closet, I settled on my usual plain Skechers that went well with just about any pair of jeans. Gavin had called me the day before and we decided there was no point in him picking me up, considering the firehouse was walking distance from my house. I would meet him there.

It was a fabulous day. The sun was shining brightly in a cloudless sky, and a gentle breeze made the early summer heat a lot more pleasurable. With my favorite lavender scarf wrapped around my neck and a pair of elegant sunglasses teetering on the top of my head, I left the house. For once I was confident and sure of myself.

Unfortunately, as I approached the fire department, my bravado began to fizzle faster than the air in a busted balloon.

What if he acts differently around his work buddies? What if he hates this stupid T-shirt? What if he doesn't think I'm sexy enough?

The other guys were all already milling around by the basketball court in front of the firehouse, chatting and throwing the ball to each other. No sign of Gavin. I struggled with the decision of whether to go inside and find him or wait for him to come out, but thankfully Gavin just appeared around the corner, a sports bag slung over his shoulder and a smile on his face. He spotted me right away and waved while sauntering across the street in my direction.

"Hi, beautiful." He searched for my lips with his and kissed me. *Okay. So we aren't hiding it from his coworkers.* I melted against him and had to brace myself with a hand around his neck for fear I would fall. Those lips were to die for. I just couldn't get enough. When we came up for air, he was smiling at me, his green eyes twinkling with mischief. "Don't look now, but the other guys are green with envy right now."

I sneaked a peek behind him and, sure enough, most of his crew was staring at us, mouths wide open, almost as if paralyzed by an alien freezing ray. I laughed against his chest—which smelled of promises of pleasure of which I was yet to partake.

"I hate to make you wait, but I've got some work

to do before the game. You're staying for the game, right?" He had taken a few steps backward, but he still held on to my hand. "We can go do something afterward."

Yes, I do want to do something for sure.

I sat down on the low wall, a premium spot to watch the game about to start. Some of the guys playfully commented on the kiss as Gavin walked into the building and then waved at me. My cheeks burned. I wasn't used to being the one envied for romantic adventures. It was kind of nice, but unnerving as well.

My mind wandered to the day I'd met Gavin and every other time since then. My very active imagination had me come up with all kinds of scenarios where our lips always ended up joined together—not to mention other equally exciting parts of our bodies. Gavin was away for a long while, but lost in my daydreaming, I didn't even notice until I heard the firemen yelling out something.

"Hurry up, bionic man." I wasn't sure who they were calling, but after counting the players already on the court, I figured it was Gavin—the only one still missing in action. The door to the building opened and the men all whistled at the same time. "Did you get enough time to put on lipstick?" Gavin emerged through the door and gave them all the finger as he trotted to the court.

My heart stopped—at least, that's how it felt. Gavin's sports shorts revealed a perfect, muscular leg and—

He has a fake leg.

I knew what I was seeing, but my brain refused to accept it. Gavin's right lower leg was a mechanical one. He ran and jumped as easily and athletically as all the other men. On a prosthetic limb. *How could that be? Why didn't he ever say anything about it?* I didn't know what to think. Him being an amputee didn't change the way I felt about him. Or did it? I was so confused.

For the rest of the game, I must have zoned out, because I couldn't remember whether anyone scored or who was winning. My head was stuck on pause. I was only half-aware when the players high-fived each other and began filing off the court. With a start, I realized Gavin was heading toward me.

What am I going to do? What am I going to say?

As it turned out, my brain decided for me. "When were you going to tell me you have a fake leg?" Whoa, not exactly sensitive or nice, but I was angry. My hands were out of control, gesturing the strong feelings assailing my heart. "Were you going to wait until we got naked in your bedroom and surprise me? Did you think I couldn't handle it? Or just thought it would be a great joke?"

Gavin grabbed my fast-moving hands and held them still against his chest. "Calm down, Ana," he whispered. "I thought you knew. Everybody knows."

"Obviously not everybody, because I had no freaking idea." Anger seethed beneath my skin, burning its way out. "How was I supposed to know? And what do you mean, everybody knows?"

"It was all over the local news. My accident. My leg, or lack thereof." Nothing was making much sense to me right now except the fact that I was furious. A boiling sense of betrayal, like bile, rose in my throat, threatening to gag me. "I'm so sorry, Ana. I really thought you knew. You're not mad at me, are you? I didn't mean to hide it from you or anything."

I didn't know how I felt about him at that moment. I was angry, that was certain. But was I mad at him or mad at myself for not having noticed? I had wondered about his funny kind of walk sometimes, but I thought it was due to some lasting injury, nothing this enormous. I couldn't be mad at him for not having a leg, but I certainly could be mad at him for keeping it a secret, couldn't I? How could he think I knew about it? I needed time and space to think about how I felt. I needed time to process it all.

"I have to go." I pulled my hands from his and turned to walk away, but he was faster, running to stand in my way. "Gavin, I don't know what to feel right now. Give me some time to think about it." He nodded, his lips twisted into a frown. "I'll call you."

I hated myself for feeling like that. What was I thinking? Wasn't Gavin the same amazing guy who had made my toes curl with his lips? Wasn't he the same exact romantic fool who had prepared my favorite sandwiches for our first date? Wasn't he the same gorgeous man I was falling in love with?

I hate this. I hate this.

As soon as I threw myself on top of my bed at home, the phone rang. It was Delta.

"How did it go? I'm surprised you're home already. I thought I'd leave you a message."

"Did you know?" I asked her, a terrible suspicion growing inside of me. Had all of them—even my best friend—been conspiring to make me look like a fool?

"Did I know what?"

"Did you know that Gavin is an amputee?" Saying the word made me feel small and petty. Why was I mad at him for something like that? "He said everyone knew. That it was in the news. Did you know about it, Delta?"

There was a gasp. "Fuck! Is he *that* Gavin?"

My voice became shrill. "You knew!"

"Now there, my friend. I didn't know that was the Gavin in the news a few years ago." She was using the tone of voice she always did when trying to appease me. "I had no way of knowing."

"Goodbye, Delta." I was done. For a moment, I wished I still had one of those old corded phones so I could slam the receiver. As it was, my clicking the off button on my cell phone didn't have quite the same dramatic effect. It would have to do for now. I was going to wallow in my own misery—justified or not—if I wanted to.

Humble Pie and Forgiveness

Gavin

My ear burned against the cell phone speaker. It was the fifth time I'd called Ana that day and probably wouldn't be the last. There was a long string of messages left for her that varied from the simple "call me" to the frantic "please, forgive me for being such an asshole." She wasn't biting. So far, I was developing a very close relationship with her voice mail. I dropped the phone on the kitchen counter and sat on one of the tall stools, my head drooping to the marble surface.

What have I done? I truly thought she knew. It was common knowledge in town that I had lost my leg in that horrible accident many years ago. I had just started my career as a fireman when it all went down the drain. Losing a limb was always traumatic, but for a twenty-four-year-old, barely out of college and starting a job that required full use of limbs, it was devastating. I went through all the stages of grief before I came to accept that I could either be a sad burden to my mother and everyone around me, or make the best of it and adjust to living with a fake leg. I chose the latter. It had been a long, painful journey, but I had made it and I was proud of myself.

Was she mad at me because I was disabled? I couldn't imagine that. Ana didn't hit me as the kind of woman who would care about something like that. So why had she been so pissed at me? Why had she run away and wouldn't talk to me? *Not hard to guess, stupid. She's mad at you because you didn't tell her.*

I snatched the phone from the counter and punched in her number again. I wasn't going to give up on her. Not now, not ever.

"You have reached Ana. Please leave a message and I'll call you back as soon as I can." It was a recording, but her voice was like a soothing balm for my aching heart.

I waited for the beep before leaving the sixth message of the day. "Ana, please call me. I'm so sorry. I didn't realize you didn't know. Let's talk about it. Please, Ana. I need—" *You.* Too early in the relationship? Possibly. Yet it was true. I needed her like the air I breathed. "I need to talk to you."

My leg looked perfectly normal, covered by jeans. The bionic parts in the joint mechanism allowed me near-normal movement. It was no wonder Ana had never suspected it.

It had been years since I'd felt this much disgust for my injury. At that moment, I wanted to be perfect and whole. I hated that. It had taken me years to like myself the way I was, and in one moment it was all gone.

The phone rang and I almost jumped out of my skin. It was my mom.

"Mom?" She always seemed to know when something was wrong. Even all the way from France where she had moved a couple years ago.

"What's wrong, Gav? Are you okay? You don't

sound okay." She had the quirky habit of answering her own questions.

"I'm fine, Mom." I wasn't fine. Not even close.

"You're not fooling anyone," she said, her voice pitching higher as it always did when she was worried. "What happened?"

I swallowed, trying to decide how much I should tell her. I didn't want to worry her too much. It was bad enough she had to go through the pain and anguish of seeing her only son almost die and later lose his leg. She'd been there the whole way, through my recovery and therapy, sitting by me the nights when grief wouldn't let me sleep, and cheering me on when I built up strength and courage to get back on my feet. My champion and my strength.

"I think I'm in love, Mom." *Where did that come from?* Until I opened my mouth, I'd had no idea that was even true.

She squealed like a little girl and I almost laughed. "My boy is finally in love. Who's the lucky girl?"

It poured like a torrent of water out of an open dam. As I spoke of my heartache, I felt lighter, relieved. My mother listened patiently, never interrupting except to ask questions. After what seemed like forever, I was finally done spilling my heart out.

"Well, son, you know what I'm going to say, don't you?"

I did. "Get back on your feet, shake yourself off, and move on." I'd heard that my whole life. "But I need her, Mom. I think I love her."

I heard a chortle from the other end of the line. "Then go tell her."

"She won't answer her phone." God, I sounded like a little boy.

"No phone. Go to her place, knock at the door." She cleared her throat. "Throw yourself at her feet if necessary. She's pissed because she thinks you hid this rather important fact from her. You have to show her you didn't do it on purpose."

I wiped my face with my hand and sighed deeply. She was right. "I'm going there right now."

"Not right now, dummy. Give her some time to simmer down. Give her a day or so. Then go there and give it all you got." She sounded as if I was about to climb into a boxing ring instead of talking to the woman who invaded my every thought and dream. "You can do it, sweetheart."

"Thank you, Mom." The darkness had lifted. She was right. I could do this. "Why did you have to move to the other side of the ocean? I could use your skinny shoulder to cry on." I chuckled.

"No ocean is wide or deep enough to separate us, son." *I love you, Mom.* "I give thanks to technology every day." She laughed in crystalline bursts of sound. "But I have to go now. My yoga class starts in fifteen minutes."

We said our goodbyes and I put down my phone. My whole being was screaming to run and throw itself into Ana's arms. It was going to be hard to wait even a few hours, much less a day or two. Hell, hard to believe I was in love.

***

Ana

The phone blinked in silence. A quick look told me there were more than twenty missed calls, and God only knew how many messages. I was torn inside as I typed away on my laptop, trying to drown my confusion and anger with words. Writing had always been my best therapy, and it was no different now. Being inside one of my stories and the lives of fictional characters was the best way I knew to escape my own problems and de-stress.

Delta had also been knocking at my door nonstop— either feeling slightly guilty for not connecting the dots, or worried that I would never come up for air again. I didn't want to talk to her. As much as I needed a shoulder to cry on, I was so confused about what to feel and how to act that I couldn't even consider talking to another human being.

The phone vibrated and danced along the top of the coffee table. I glanced at it briefly. *Shit! It's Mom.* I had to pick up.

"Honey, are you okay?" My mother's half-hysterical voice pierced my ear. She had always had a flair for the dramatic and loved to make a mountain out of a molehill. What was she going on about now? "Delta called me last night and told me you've been locked in your house for over a week now. What's going on?"

Delta, you traitor. You'll pay for this.

"Delta is exaggerating," I lied, gulping a bit too loudly. "I've been busy with a new novel, that's all. Nothing to worry about."

"I know how you are, duckling." Oh my God, I hated when she called me that. It made me feel like I was ten years old all over again. My mother had never accepted the fact I was a grown woman. An almost middle-aged woman. "Something happened and you're hiding from the world like you always do. Have you showered? Eaten?"

"Mom!" Now I really sounded like a kid. Why did she bring out that side of me? "I'm not a slob or stupid."

"Well, there was that time when the boy you liked told the whole school you were a four-eyed piglet." *Thanks, Mom, for bringing that up.* "Remember?" How could I forget? It was one of the most humiliating times of my whole life. "You went for almost two weeks without brushing your hair and refused to get dressed and eat."

"I was fifteen, Mom." My protest was heartfelt and loud. "I have grown a bit since then."

"Anyway, I should come over and make sure you're getting your meals."

Hell, no. The last thing I needed was my

overprotective mother hovering over me as I was trying to figure out what exactly was bothering me about this whole thing.

"No, Mom. I have a few deadlines and I can't have visitors right now." I could already see her, bags in hand, running through the hallways of the Sea-Tac airport as if running away from a raging fire—oh, shit, why did I have to think about fire? "You can't come. Not now, Mom. Promise me you won't come."

"Are you sure? Are you going to eat regular meals?" *Oh, boy.* "And take showers every day? I worry about you, duckling."

After promising her a million times that I wouldn't starve or allow myself to turn into a bag lady, she sounded appeased and hung up. I sighed deeply. Talking to my mom always exhausted me. I loved her dearly, but she could be so overbearing. And weird. Let's face it. My mother was weird.

The phone vibrated again and I picked up without thinking. "Mom, I promised you—"

"Who are you calling mom?" It was Delta. "What the hell is going on, girl? I'm coming over and you better open that fucking door."

I was about to protest but she hung up on me, and I knew she would be at my doorstep in no time. Better put a comb through my rat's nest or I'd never hear the end of it.

In front of the mirror, I wondered over my puffy eyes—been crying a lot—and my splotchy skin. I looked a fright and didn't feel any better. Confusion clouded my judgment. I didn't know what to think. On one hand, guilt assailed me: how could I be angry at Gavin for being an amputee? But was I mad at him because of that or because he had never told me, because he was *afraid* of telling me? Yes, he claimed he thought I knew, but I couldn't bring myself to fully believe that. Had he not trusted me enough to not care about the fact he was missing a limb? How dare he? How dare he think I was that shallow?

The doorbell rang in a rapid sequence of squeaks. *I have to fix that bell.* Delta stormed into my house, umbrella in hand and an angry frown on her lips. "You are really pissing me off. What did I or the poor fireman do to make you so mad? Can you at least tell me that?"

I followed her into the living room and perched on the arm of my sofa, avoiding her eyes. I wasn't sure what to say, having just now realized what was bothering me.

"Well?" She sat on my couch, her lips pursed and her hands primly on her lap.

The truth came pouring out of me faster than I was even aware of it. All my insecurities had come back to bite me in the ass. It wasn't Gavin or the fact that he walked on a fake leg. It was that deep doubt in my heart that maybe, just maybe, he hadn't trusted me enough to share it with me. The fear he didn't think well enough of me to believe I wouldn't care. That I would love him no matter what.

"Love? Did you just say you love him?" Delta's eyes were open wide, round like tiny full moons, and if it weren't for the fact I was so upset, I would have laughed.

I guess I did say that. Is it true though? Am I falling for this gentle, beautiful, and courageous man I have known for such a short time?

"Damn it, Delta. I don't know what I'm feeling anymore." I buried my face in my hands. "I'm so confused."

For once, my loud friend was quiet. For a moment, at least. "If you're confused, how do you think he's feeling?" *No idea.* I had been too preoccupied with my own feelings to spare too long on his. A wave of guilt washed over me. Shit. *How can I be so callous?* "Here you are all into the idea of you as a couple, and then he shows you his disability and you bolt, mad at him."

I was horrified as the full ramifications of my actions took roots. "Oh my God, I can't believe I didn't even think about that." I slapped my knees in anger. "I'm a mess. I thought I had put this whole relationship fear behind me, but apparently, my heartaches of the past are not as buried as I hoped they were."

Delta drew me into her generous arms and patted me on the back as if trying to burp me. "What are you going to do then?"

What can I do? Apologize, of course. And hope Gavin was big enough to accept it and not hate me too much for it. I sniffled and straightened up.

"Time to eat some crow."

I was not above apologizing, but it was humiliating to think I had been so freaking unfair to him just because I was unsure of myself and afraid of getting hurt all over again. My female characters were not at all like me. They were brave and audacious, sure of themselves and accepting no crap from anyone. I, on the other hand, was always afraid of being stepped on and not having the spunk to do anything about it other than cry. Time to dust myself off and move on.

Under Delta's watchful eye, I stood up, took a deep breath, and punched in his number on my phone.

Gavin picked up on the second ring. "Ana, thank God! I was so worried."

He was worried? Not mad or hurt? I fell in love with him a little more right then.

"I need to talk to you," I managed to say. "Apologize, really—"

"Apologize for what? You have nothing to be sorry for." *What? Is he serious?* "I'm the one who should be apologizing. I just assumed you knew. It must have been a shock."

An overwhelming urge to hug him took over me. "No, no—you did nothing wrong." I needed to see him. Now. "Can I come over?"

Delta was already by the door when I hung up, my purse in her hand and a smile on her face. "He seems like a lovely man. Not all guys are out to yank your heart out and eat it, you know."

I grabbed my umbrella and smiled back at her. "Thanks for coming over and slapping me back to sanity. You're the best." I crossed the space between us and hugged her. "Love you, Delta. I owe you big."

Delta laughed and playfully slapped my cheeks. "I won't let you forget that." She was already on her way out when she spun around to face me one last time. "Ever!" She turned around again, umbrella opened over her head, and cackled like the Wicked Witch of the West.

Fire and Love

Gavin

Ana was coming over and I was moving around like Duffy Duck in a panic, picking up dirty clothes and dishes, fluffing pillows—yes, I actually fluffed my couch cushions—and spraying the air with something I thought was lavender scent but turned out to be bug spray. I must have checked myself in the mirror a hundred times, but saw no difference. My face was as always and my hair—well, I didn't have enough hair for it to be disheveled. At the last minute, I decided to change my shirt, convinced it smelled of something strange. I was stupid nervous.

"She wanted to talk, so that's a good sign." *Oh, shit. I'm talking to myself now.* "Right? It *has* to be a good thing." I paced around the room, acutely aware of my fake limb. I hadn't thought about it in a long time, but now that it was at the center of my biggest problem again, it was all I could think about.

Twisting my hands, I dropped into the comfort of the couch. I reached out, grabbed a cushion, and sank my face in it before screaming and growling like a bear. How was it possible I was so fucking in love with this woman I couldn't take her out of my thoughts? She inhabited my dreams—good and bad—and reigned over my days. My whole body tensed up at the mere thought of her. I wanted her. No, I needed her.

My phone vibrated in my pocket. Jackson. Was he psychic or something?

"Can't talk now, Jacks." *The woman of my dreams is coming over.* "What's going on?"

"Just checking on you. You've been looking a little worse for wear." He sounded worried. "Are you sick?"

I scratched my head and sighed loudly. "Shit, Jacks. I am sick—lovesick." I hated how it sounded. I wasn't in high school anymore, pining over some cheerleader who wouldn't give me the time of day. I was a thirty-one-year-old man who was past his time for wild crushes. "I feel so fucking stupid."

Jackson's laughter rolled to my ear. "We're all stupid when it comes to love and women, dude." He laughed even harder. "I think that's the definition of love where men are concerned: something that makes you an utter idiot."

"What do I do then? I can't get Ana out of my head." *Do I really want to?* The truth was that as much as my life was in an uproar thanks to her, it was also a lot more interesting, richer in flavor and texture. I didn't think I would want it any other way.

"Do what we all do—go with the flow. Enjoy the ride, man. As much as I complain about my wife, I don't know what I would do without her." My friend went silent for a moment. "If you love her, go for it, dude. What the hell is stopping you anyway? She's beautiful and smart, even though she finds you attractive." He chuckled at his own joke.

"Thanks, Jacks. She's coming over in a few. Wish me luck."

As soon as I pressed the off button on my phone, I heard a noise outside my door. *Shit. This is it. Ana must be here.* The moment of reckoning had arrived. I swallowed hard, stood up, and marched to open the door.

***

Ana

Are you ever going to knock on the door?

I had been standing by his door for at least five minutes, my hand staged to ring the bell but not quite making it there. Now that I was there, my bravado had left me. My legs shook, and my face burned in embarrassment. I was so ashamed I had reacted like I did. It was much like that nightmare of walking naked in the office or classroom. My not-so-nice side had been exposed to the man I was developing very strong feelings for. He must think I was an idiot, getting spooked by the fact he was an amputee. I couldn't stand it. The guilt was like an elephant sitting on my chest.

Before I collected myself enough to knock or ring the bell, the door opened and Gavin's handsome face appeared. His soft, and yet vibrant, eyes locked with mine, and my whole body vibrated. Fighting the urge to throw myself into his arms, I bit my lip so hard I tasted blood.

"I'm so disappointed in myself, Gavin." I had found my voice. "I'm so afraid of being hurt I never stopped to think that I was being so terribly disrespectful to you."

He took a hesitant step forward. "It was my fault. I should have told you."

I love you. Oh, shit, I love this man.

My chest was about to explode. "No, it was not your fault." Urgently, I added, "And please don't think I ran because you're disabled—which is totally the wrong description of what you are. You're amazing. You're beautiful and brave and—" *Oh no. Here I go again—babbling like an idiot.*

Gavin didn't let me finish. In one fluid move, he gathered me in his arms and squeezed me against him. When his lips took mine, I went limp within his embrace. His taste was intoxicating, and electricity ran through my veins, unchecked and exciting.

"Maybe we should step inside." We were still standing in front of his door. "The neighbors may get curious." He chuckled, and I detected a tremor of nervousness in his voice. *Is he as anxious about this as I am?*

Still hanging on to him, I stepped inside his apartment and kicked the door closed behind me. My body was glued to his and it was heaven. I sighed against his mouth, and he kissed me again. Deeply and completely, his tongue inviting mine for a sensual dance that ignited a roaring fire inside of me. It had been too long. I had almost forgotten how amazing it was to allow yourself to drown in the pleasure of someone's loving touch.

"What are we doing, Gavin?" I managed to ask when we came up for air. I knew what I felt, but I needed to hear his side of it. I had never been the kind of girl who had sex just for the fun of it. It was too easy for me to get too involved, too quickly. No one-night stands for me, no casual hookups. I had nothing against them; I just couldn't handle them. I needed to know that Gavin was at least a little invested in this relationship before—

"I don't know about you, but I'm about to make mad hot love to you," he whispered against my lips, sending a million shivers of pleasure all the way down to my toes.

I giggled and caressed his face, delighting in the slightly scratchy texture of his day-old stubble. "I mean the two of us. Is this a one-time thing or are we starting something?" I hated that I sounded so needy, but I had to know.

He chuckled. "I'm hoping this is just the first time of many epic future make-out sessions." Then he sobered up and lowered his voice. "And the beginning of a beautiful relationship."

My insides oozed and sizzled at his words. Beautiful relationship indeed. "Don't be so cocky. What makes you think it will be epic?"

In a sudden movement, he scooped me off the ground, his lips descending on mine again. "Why don't I show you instead?" I wrapped my legs around his waist and suckled on his lower lip as he carried me deeper into his apartment and into his bedroom. "Be prepared to be awed."

I laughed, my nose buried in the crook of his neck, delighting in his scent. "So sure of yourself, aren't you?"

He dropped me gently on his bed, where I lay back, supporting myself on my elbows. "They don't call me bionic man for no reason."

A resurfacing of my earlier mortification at how I had reacted made my cheeks burn hot, and I hid my eyes. He crawled over me and kissed me again, erasing my doubts and guilt. I could have lost myself in that kiss and never come up for air or food. My hands were itching for action, so I fumbled with the buttons of his shirt, desperate to feel his skin. He stopped me and took it off himself, shrugging it off his arm with a grunt of frustration. The damned thing was stuck.

"The bionic man can't even get undressed on his own," I quipped, pulling his sleeve free and throwing the shirt over my head. By all the angels in heaven, he was even more beautiful than I thought. His chest was strong, lined with well-defined muscles and—scars. They marred his skin from the left shoulder to the center in two irregular, almost parallel lines. I traced them, and he shivered under my touch.

"More souvenirs from the accident," he explained. "Do they bother you?" He held my gaze.

I shook my head. I found those scars as sexy as the rest of him. They were part of who he was and a reminder of what he had been through. I flipped him around so I was now on top, and answered by tracing the scars again, this time with my lips and my tongue. He moaned and trembled, and the pleasure of knowing the effect I had on him almost overwhelmed me.

He held the edges of my T-shirt and pulled until it flew freely over both our heads to fall on the floor somewhere. His green gaze scanned my exposed skin and he blinked, the corner of his mouth arching into a half smile. We switched positions again and he made a big production of removing my old wear-around-the-house bra. Any other time, I would have been embarrassed, but this was Gavin. I wanted to share the mess that was me totally and completely. I didn't want any secrets between us—large or small. I wanted him to love me wholly, not just the made-for-public-consumption parts.

With the offensive clothing article removed, I was now mentally urging him to use those amazing lips of his. He obliged, latching them around my breast, gently at first and then hungrily. I wanted more of him. So much more.

"Can we get rid of those pants?"

He hesitated briefly and I wondered whether he was nervous about me seeing his prosthesis up close. It didn't hold him back for more than a few seconds though. Sliding off the edge of the bed, Gavin stood and rushed to remove his jeans, allowing me a full view of his imperfect but oh-so-amazing body.

My fireman was indeed very real, all hard muscle and sinew. As he stood there, bare and vulnerable, I realized I couldn't give a hoot about his fake leg. I loved every inch of him, visible and invisible, whole or broken. I was in love.

He pulled on my yoga pants—God, I looked like a slob—and it was my turn to bare it all. Gavin's breathing sped up to match mine, and I couldn't handle it anymore. I had to have him, his skin against mine, hardness against softness.

Sitting on the edge of the bed, I worked my way from his chest to his neck with my lips, my hands flattened against his bottom, shivering in anticipation of how he would feel inside of me. He swelled against me and I whimpered in yearning.

"Okay, fireman," I said, my voice thick with desire. "Let's put out this fire."

***

Gavin

Holy mother of God, she felt good. Her softness against my hard muscle was intoxicating. The heat of her silky skin made my own explode in goose bumps of excitement. I swelled against her, and every time she moaned or whimpered against my lips, I swelled further. An explosion was gathering momentum inside me as every muscle in my body tensed and shook in anticipation of what was yet to come.

"Are you going to make me wait all night?" Her whisper, a blow of soft air against my ear, made me shiver from head to toe. "I need you."

Not that I needed any encouragement, but her words fanned the fire in me. I pushed her gently onto her back and devoured every inch of her naked body with my eyes. There was so much understated beauty in her. The tantalizing fullness of her breasts, the subtle curve of her hips and how they narrowed down to her inner thighs. I caressed her, brushing my hand from her neck down to her breasts where I lingered for a moment, relishing the reaction I stirred. With a feathery touch, I continued my trek down her body, flat belly, and lower. She wiggled and arched against my exploring fingers, moaning.

"I've been dreaming of this moment, Ana." Might as well confess. I hadn't slept in days thinking of how she would feel beneath me, under the probing of my hands and my lips. Her legs hung awkwardly over the edge of the bed, so I scooped her up until she was fully on it, magnificent in her birthday suit. I was so hard I truly thought I might explode, but I wanted this moment to last. My body said, "Take her now." But my heart said, "Take it easy."

I slid my hands up her legs and gently pried them apart to touch her again. She made a tiny, guttural sound that almost made me lose control. I wouldn't last much longer. With my blood flowing wild in my veins, I followed my fingers with my lips and tasted her. She screamed as my tongue touched her warm folds, and I gripped the bed coverings in an attempt to stay cool. Impossible feat. I was burning inside and out, hotter than the air in a house on fire.

"Do you have a condom?" I was so intoxicated I was not sure where the question had come from. Ana had pulled me away from her thighs and was looking at me, desire shining in her eyes. "Do you have protection, Gavin?"

Like a fool I nodded, and rolled off the bed to get one from my stash in the dresser. My clumsy fingers fumbled with the wrapper and I almost dropped the damned thing.

"Let me do it."

Yes, please.

I handed it to her and rolled back on top of the bed, next to her. With much defter fingers than mine, my petite writer ripped the package open and removed the much-needed item from it. She turned slightly on her side and pushed me flat on the bed while she rolled the condom over the one part of me that seemed the most out of control. I was about to sit up when she pushed me down again and straddled me. In maddeningly slow movements, she gyrated against my arousal, her hands resting on my chest. Unexpectedly, she winked and stopped moving. I protested.

"Now, fireman," she said, a mischievous little smile on her lips, "the best things come to those who wait. Patiently."

The little minx was teasing me. She knew I was so close to the edge it wouldn't take much to push me over.

Ana, supported by her hands against me, lifted herself up from my body and then slid herself onto me—so slowly the pleasure was as intense as the agony.

"Holy shit, that feels—" What? Amazing? Out of this world? She was the writer. I had no adjectives to describe what I felt right then. I flattened my hands against her buttocks and pressed her harder, my hips rising to meet her. It was everything I'd dreamed of and then some.

Our bodies moved together in that frantic, intimate

dance only two lovers can share. She held me inside of her, sheathing me with welcoming warmth, soothing and arousing all at once. I cupped her perfect breasts with my hands and shivered in delight when she pressed against them, urging me to go further, rocking back and forth on top of me. It wasn't long until the stars in the sky descended into my eyes and I yelled out in the ecstasy of release. She shook against me, her head thrown back. I slid my hands down to her waist and held her down, wanting our contact to be even more intimate, not wanting to break apart.

Ana, flushed and smiling, collapsed on top of me, her head on my chest. Our bodies still connected, we came down from our high flight together. *Can she hear my beating heart? It's beating for her.*

"Does it bother you?" I bit my tongue. Now was not the time to ask this. She mumbled a question against my chest. "My leg. Does it bother you in any way?"

She fluttered her lips across my skin, making me tremble in pleasure again. "Don't be stupid. Why would it bother me?"

"It's a turnoff for some women." I should know. There had been a few awkward moments in my dating life that involved averted eyes and sudden excuses of "I forgot I have a thing tonight."

"Are you kidding me?" Ana laughed and lifted her heart-shaped face to me. "What self-respecting woman would even notice your leg amid all that Greek god body of yours?"

That made me laugh. It was the first time anyone called me a Greek god look-alike. I kind of liked it.

Ana slid her hands down and around my sides and clutched my buttocks. "You're a hot number, fireman. And here I was, wanting to write about a regular, everyday guy."

Her hands were sending shivers down my spine. The great kind.

"I'm a regular guy."

"There's nothing *regular* about you, Gavin." I wanted to be special, to be the only one for her. I wanted to fill her every night and sleep next to her until morning. "You're not only deliciously sexy, but you're also an amazing human being."

My lips stretched into what I was sure was a silly smile. Her heart pounded in unison with mine and I almost said it. Instead, I uttered, "You're the most beautiful woman I've ever met." *And I love you. I love you with every fiber of my body, heart, and soul.*

Coffee and Ducklings

Ana

The doorbell rang and I almost jumped out of my skin. I wasn't ready yet. Gavin was coming over and I wanted to have a surprise for him, a sexy surprise. Without delay, I shrugged off the rest of my clothes and tied the apron I had bought the day before over my very naked body. My frilly black-and-pink body protector barely covered my chest, but it demanded—in big curly pink letters—Kiss the World's Worst Cook. Considering the time Gavin had first come over to my house, I thought it was very appropriate. I rushed to the door, tucking in a rogue boob that kept spilling out from behind the apron.

Holy shit! It's Mom! What was she doing here? She was supposed to be in Seattle. Good thing I had looked through the peephole before opening the door. My mom, arms crossed in frustration, stood right behind my door, the only thing preventing her from getting an eyeful of her slutty daughter wearing close to nothing. *Oh my God. Got to get dressed quickly.* "Wait up, Mom. I'm coming."

After slipping into my discarded clothes faster than even the Flash ever would, I ran to open the door, my panties—*did I put them on backwards?*—insisting on giving me an irritating wedgie and my hair in disarray. Mom didn't look too happy.

"What in heaven's name took so long?" She strode purposefully into my house, her fire-eye trained on me.

My mother was still a beautiful woman, her brown hair streaked with silver and her blue eyes as bright and lively as when she was a young woman. She also had a knack for elegance in the way she dressed and carried herself—the gene obviously having missed me altogether. I often wondered whether my baby sister would have been more like her, well put-together and gorgeous. But we didn't speak of Yvette. Ever. She was the heartbreak that had never healed, and would be taboo until such time tears didn't immediately threaten to run down both our faces.

"Mom, you live on the west coast. Why are you here?" I looked around her for suitcases. "Where is your luggage?"

"I left them at the hotel." Uh-oh, her voice didn't bode well. "I'm moving back so I can be close to you." I must have frowned, because she added, "Don't give me that look. And why in heaven's name did it take you so long to open the door?"

"You look nice." My pitiful attempt at distracting her didn't work, and she gifted me with her famous X-ray look. *I'm so easy.* "All right, Mom. I'm sorry. I wasn't dressed yet."

"It's almost four o'clock in the afternoon. You were still in pj's?" I sighed, resigned to enduring the usual lecture about personal hygiene. My mother seemed to be under the impression that I was a slob, when in fact I was a very clean and tidy person. It was the rare day when I didn't get up before seven and wasn't totally dressed and ready to go by eight.

"I was changing to go—" Shit. She'd trapped me into telling her the almost truth. "To go on a date."

Her perfect face lit up in a smile. "A date? You're dating again?" I was startled by her tone of voice. I had only heard my mother squeal twice—once when she found a squirrel nesting in our laundry basket, and when Yvette had won first prize for a dance competition years ago. But squeal she did then. "Oh, sweet duckling, I'm so happy for you."

Before I could step aside, I was enveloped in a bear hug. "Mom, I can't breathe." She loosened up the hold a bit. "I can't believe you're this excited about me dating."

She pushed me away and arched her beautifully shaped eyebrows in disbelief. "You've been divorced for more than two years and not once have you gone out on a date. Of course, I'm delighted. I was beginning to think I'd never be a grandma."

Great! I'd just started dating Gavin and she was already getting me pregnant. This was why I didn't share many life events with my mother. "We just went on a couple dates. It's not like we're making plans for the future yet." Well, I was, but then again, I always did. Thus the lack of dating after my failed marriage.

Her arm looped through mine, she led me to the couch. "So tell me, who's this guy who finally got your nose out of the books and into real life again?"

Resistance was futile. My mom was as relentless as any Borg, and she wouldn't take no for an answer. "His name is Gavin. He's a fireman." I would leave out the fact he was rather wealthy for now, or she would be making reservations for our wedding reception. "He's a very nice man."

She looked up at me, squinting. "Cute? Like the guys in your stories?"

"What do you know about my stories?" I had been very diligent at keeping my mother away from my romances. I didn't want to find out she hated my writing and, most of all, I didn't want her reading my sexy love scenes. I wanted her to think of me as the pure little girl I once was. Not the one imagining the sex in the boudoir of my fictional characters. "You haven't read them, have you?"

"Don't get your panties all in a twist, girl." Too late. They were seriously twisted and giving me a rash by now. "I confess. I have read one or two of your romances."

My face was on fire. "Oh my God! How embarrassing." I hid my face in my hands.

"Come on, duckling. Did you think I wouldn't read your books?" *Yes, I did. I really did.* "You're my daughter and I'm very proud of what you've accomplished." I still couldn't look at her. She giggled. "I'm also glad to know you're not totally ignorant of the bedroom arts."

"Mom!" Now, I would have to dig up a hole and bury myself in it forever.

"Stop playing coy. Is he cute?" I peeked at her through a gap in my fingers. "Your fireman. Is he big and muscular?"

I moaned, wiping my face with my hand. "He's a real guy, Mom. Not a romance book character. He's handsome, and yes, built in all the right places but— he's a normal, nice guy."

"You act like you can't be muscular *and* nice." Why was I wasting my time arguing with my mother, the most obstinate woman on the planet? "When do I meet him?"

As if on cue, the doorbell rang. *Shit, it's Gavin.* This was not good at all.

"Mom, you have to be cool and leave Gavin alone, you hear?" I could hear the desperation in my voice. This was going to be painful.

"Don't be silly, duckling. I would never embarrass you." Right. And the Pope wasn't Catholic.

I flung myself toward the door, my underwear still

giving me trouble. "And don't call me duckling in front of him, please."

As soon as I opened the door and met Gavin's amazing green eyes, I forgot my mom was just behind me. I sighed deeply, my whole body relaxing at the sight of him and my mind immediately fleeing to the memories of our one epic night of lovemaking.

"Hi, beautiful." In one fluid stride, Gavin drew me into his arms and kissed me.

His mouth tasted exotic and forbidden, exhilarating and— My mom! My mother was watching me as I stuck my tongue down this handsome man's throat. I pushed him away forcefully. Gavin stumbled and had to brace himself against the wall.

"Gavin, this is my mom, Elaine Mathews. She just got here from Seattle." I wiped a hand over my swollen lips, and a shiver went down my spine and into my girly parts as I remembered his taste. Gavin stared at the smiling woman on the couch. "Mom, this is Gavin."

She stood up, her hand stretched out in front of her. "My daughter's boyfriend." *Just kill me now.* "So nice to meet you." A rather stunned Gavin took her hand and shook it. "A fireman, are you?"

He glanced over at me and I shrugged, giving up on any pretense of control. "My mom decided to surprise me and showed up at my door a little bit ago." Catching me with my pants down. Literally.

"Nice to meet you, Mrs. Mathews." Gavin smiled, finally recovering his wits.

"Call me Elaine. So, where are you taking my daughter?" Gavin choked. We hadn't been planning to go anywhere farther than my bedroom. Maybe not even that far. "Oh, *that* kind of date. I better leave you then. Don't want to embarrass my duckling anymore." *Too late for that, Mom.*

Gavin jumped into action. "No, no. You just took me by surprise. I was going to take Ana to Grind N Crepe." *Sweet, sweet man.* "Care to join us?" *Stupid, stupid man.*

For once, my mother did the right thing. "That's very sweet of you, but I can't stay. I have a hair appointment on the other side of town." She winked at me and blood rushed to my face. "Love you, duckling."

We said our goodbyes, and I exhaled loudly as the door closed behind her. "So sorry, Gavin. I didn't know she would show up." I spotted my sexy apron draped over the back of a chair and laughed. "I had a surprise lined up for you, but—"

He hooked his arm around my waist and pulled me against him. "Did it involve us getting naked?" I laughed against his strong chest. "It did, didn't it? I like that kind of surprise. Can we recreate it?"

"I just can't. Not after having my mother sitting there." Her face was still etched in my mind, and her voice ringing in my ears. "Maybe we should go to the Grind N Crepe instead."

Gavin chuckled, dropped a kiss on my nose, and let me go. "Coffee shop it is, then."

I turned my back on him and headed to my room. "I have something I need to do first." Like turning my panties the right side around. The wedgie was killing me.

"I'll be here." His voice reached my ears with the power of a caress. "But hurry up… duckling."

Awesome!

***

Gavin

"Ana, did you fall asleep or something?" My girl had a dreamy, dazed look in her dark eyes, as if her mind had wondered far away. "Duckling—?"

Her eyes rounded and focused on me. She licked her lips and slowly shook herself out of whatever trance she had fallen into. Not for the first time I gushed over her beautiful, always messy black hair and full, sensual lips.

"What?"

I laughed. "You were in la-la land. Where did you go?"

Much to my surprise, she blushed furiously. "My writer's imagination takes me to weird places sometimes." Hiding her eyes, she busied herself taking a long sip of her by now cold coffee. We'd become regulars at the Grind N Crepe since the day her mother had shown up at her house by surprise.

"Did it involve us in some level of nakedness?" I had to ask. Her face and neck were beet red. "Or at least one of us?"

She choked on the coffee, coughing and almost spilling the rest of the mug's contents on the table. Still chuckling, I stood up and moved behind her, gently patting her back. It took her a while to regain her composure.

"You seem a little uncomfortable with the idea. Not sure why, considering we have *been* naked together already." I was just teasing her, seeing how far I could go before she got mad at me. Her walnut eyes became fiery when she was furious, giving her a sexy-as-hell aura of beauty.

Ana looked around us as if afraid somebody had overheard me, but the other patrons were too busy with their own conversations to pay us any attention.

"Well? Was it?" I was not going to let it go that easily.

With a great sigh, she lifted her eyes to mine. "It may have involved some state of undress—I'm a romance writer after all. Sometimes I tend to see things through my writer's lens."

"Ah-ha! I knew it." I relished my victory—over what, I was not quite sure. "Were we having fun?"

Her lips turned up into a wicked smile, and my coy romance writer transformed into more of a vixen. "*I* certainly was," she said with a wink. "The things you were doing to me—"

Shit. Now I need a cold shower. Still standing behind the chair, I leaned against her and bent down to plant a kiss behind her ear. I was rewarded with a subtle moan.

I whispered in her ear, "We could go to my place for a while and reenact your dream." *Or create new ones.*

Ana looked up at me and nodded, flushed again. I pulled back in preparation for our departure, but she never quite made it out of the chair. Someone squealed and called my girlfriend's name, bringing both of us down from our sexy cloud. *Who is that?*

"Mom?" Holy shit, it was her mother. This woman sure seemed to have a gift to show up at the most inconvenient times. "What are you doing here?"

"I came to see my duckling, of course." Without waiting for an invitation, she sat down on my chair. Where was I supposed to sit? I decided to stay where I was—with my unruly bottom half hidden behind Ana.

"But you just came to see me a few days ago." I could hear the guilt in Ana's feeble protest and I smiled. It was a feeling I could totally understand. My mother, as amazing as she was, always seemed to be able to bring on that guilt, that weird, unjustified sense of wrongdoing. As if I had been caught with my hand in the cookie jar. Which at this time was quite appropriate—I was not moving from my hiding place anytime soon.

"Well, honey, that's the thing with mothers. We always miss our children." She looked inside my cup and frowned. "This smells awful. What is it?"

My eyebrows shot upwards. "An espresso."

She wrinkled her nose in disgust. "Revolting." With a wave of her hand, she called the waiter and ordered a hot herbal tea. "I haven't touched coffee in years."

Mrs. Mathews was a beautiful woman like her daughter, but very different. In fact, it was hard to imagine the two as related at all. Where Ana was dark, her mother was light. Ana was short and curvy; her mom was tall and slim like a classic Hollywood star. My girlfriend favored casual, comfortable clothes; her mom was the elegant type, all tight-fitting clothes and high heels.

"So, what are you two kids planning?" *I didn't realize we were planning anything other than a trip to my place.* But she seemed to think otherwise.

"Excuse me? What do you mean, Mrs. Mathews?"

"Call me Elaine, please." The waiter came to our table and the sweet scent of the hot tea reached my nose. "I mean, what are you planning to do about your relationship? Is it casual? Is it serious?"

"Mom!" Ana practically yelled, her ivory complexion turning scarlet once again.

"I know you write about a lot of *casual* affairs in your romances." The word casual was uttered with a certain amount of emphasis. "Is that what this is?"

In spite of myself—and my commiseration with Ana about her nosy mother—I wanted to hear her answer. What *was* this we had? I knew I was in love with this tiny, curvy, romantic woman, but how did she feel about me? Did she love me back, or was I a mere distraction?

"Mother, this is neither the place nor the time to have this discussion," Ana said through clenched teeth.

"You haven't decided yet, have you?" *Well, we haven't talked about it.* "Oops, seems I have stuck a foot in my mouth. Sorry. Forget I said anything. Let's just drink our tea and go on with our lives."

Easy for her to say. Now I was wondering. I wanted to know what role I had in Ana's life. Was I just research for one of her romances? I couldn't handle it if that was the case. I was head over heels in love with her. I wanted so much more than just casual sex and a date here and there; I wanted a lifetime together.

My mouth went dry. Without realizing, I had given my heart—the one thing I selfishly and fiercely protected—to this tiny writer. And, even more surprising, it felt good. For once, I wasn't afraid of being tied down, not being able to live my life free of constraints. For once, I welcomed being vulnerable and weak. I was all right being myself, as long as it was with her.

Ice Cream and Tears

Ana

My male character was not turning out quite the way I thought he would. The quest for the "real man" was not going well—at least not on paper. After sending out a couple of surveys to my readers, it seemed obvious that the preference leaned toward a buff and unrealistically gorgeous man. Who was I to argue with the wonderful people who read my books?

In real life though, I had found a real man, and I was head over heels happy I had. Gavin was handsome, but was no Adonis; strong and muscular, but not the Rock. He was perfect. Perfectly lovely. My crazy romantic mind was already making plans and dreaming up all sorts of life events together. Try as I may, I couldn't keep my feet solidly on the ground. I was too much of a dreamer, too much of a romantic.

Gavin had called me first thing that morning. If the

phone's ring jarred my still asleep brain, his voice, soft and warm, soothed my nerves and brought a smile to my face.

"How's my duckling?" He had latched on to my mom's terrible term of endearment and made it his. Except I didn't hate it when *he* called me that. On my mom's lips, the word sounded childish and indulgent, but on his, it sounded sexy and flattering.

His duckling was being a lazy bum that morning. I peeked at the alarm clock and moaned. "It's only six thirty, Gavin."

"Never too early to get up and enjoy life." It was his usual comment every time I or anyone else complained about something meaningless like that. His accident had no doubt left him with a renewed love for life, a willingness to embrace even the annoying moments the day-by-day threw at us. "I want you to come to the station today."

"Why? Do you want me to set the training tower on fire for you?" All I had to do was try to cook something in it. Gavin and I were the perfect pair. I set things on fire—accidentally, but still—and he put them out. I giggled, amused by my own drowsy thoughts.

Gavin laughed. "I bet you could do that quite easily, but no. I have something to show you."

Remembering the recent incident with the apron and my mom, I immediately burned from head to toe. "You're not planning on greeting me by the fire truck in nothing but a tie, are you? Not that I'd mind, but I'd prefer it without an audience."

"You have a dirty mind—I like it." He cleared his throat, as if the idea I'd just planted in his brain was causing him some trouble. "But unfortunately it's nothing sexy. Will you come?"

My usual slow awakening be damned! I jumped out of bed and got dressed so fast I must have broken some record. In no time, I was out the door, makeup reasonably in place, my hair propped up into a messy bun, wearing a pair of comfortable black palazzo pants and a flowing, loose lavender tunic. I was already at the end of the driveway when I realized I had no shoes. Two minutes later, and sporting my glittering slides, I was running down the street like a madwoman.

As soon as I turned the corner and had a visual of the firehouse, I noticed a group of the men gathered by the basketball hoop. They were all crouching down and looking at something in the center. I spotted Gavin and my heart did a little dance in my chest. He was the only one standing, and just as I locked eyes on him, he saw me. I didn't walk. I flew, my feet barely touching the ground, into his generous arms.

"Duckling, you're here," he whispered against my lips.

Yes, I'm here and always will be. Uh-oh, there it was—my cheesy, romantic soul.

"What was it you wanted to show me?" Better distract myself from his tasty lips, sexy neck, and everything that came below it.

He gently pulled me away and pointed at the ground where the other guys were all crouched in a circle. In the middle, a hairy mess of honey wiggled about, a tiny wet black snout sniffing the firemen's clothes. A puppy! A cute golden retriever.

"He's so cute!" For a moment, I forgot my man and dove into the huddle to pet the adorable hairball. "Oh, he's so sweet." The puppy jumped on my knees and licked my face vigorously while I laughed in delight. I had always loved dogs. "What's his name?"

"Honey," one of the guys said. "It's a girl."

"I thought you'd get a kick out of her." It was my sweet Gavin. He smiled and winked at me, obviously pleased I was enjoying myself.

The frolicking with the dog went on for a while. Eventually, Gavin and some of the other guys went inside to accomplish some work while I stayed outdoors with the dog and a couple of Gavin's colleagues. Honey had exhausted me, and my legs were sore from squatting to her level for so long. I stretched and sat on the low wall just as one of the men attached a leash to the puppy and took her on a walk.

I sighed, tired but happy. It had been such a great week. "Gavin is great." I wasn't sure why I felt I needed to establish that fact with his friends, but he was all I had in my brain of late.

"He's an amazing guy," one of the guys, Alan, said. "I still can't believe how he bounced back from that freaky accident."

Justin, the other fireman who had stayed outside with me, nodded. "Yeah, it was bad. We all thought he was a goner."

So far, I had only heard bits and pieces about the accident that had caused Gavin the loss of his leg. I was curious, but couldn't gather the courage to ask Gavin himself, not wanting to bring up painful memories.

"How did it happen exactly? The accident."

Alan traded a glance with Justin, as if asking for permission to tell the tale. I noticed Justin's tiny nod before Alan turned back to me.

"It was terrifying. Gavin had been out with friends, celebrating a rescue they had made the night before." Alan lowered his voice and glanced briefly at the door to the building. "There had been some heavy drinking and he really shouldn't have been driving, but—" My heart must have stopped, because I couldn't breathe for a second. Gavin was driving drunk? "The car ended up wrapped around a tree. Gavin somehow managed to survive, but Bill was dead on impact." *Oh my God! There was someone else in the car with him.* "Bill was Gavin's best friend and mentor in the fire department. Once he was conscious and out of the woods, Gavin almost crashed again when he found out about Bill."

"The accident happened because of drunk driving?" I couldn't be sure my words were audible, or if I had just uttered them inside my head.

Justin exchanged another look with Alan and they both nodded, their eyes avoiding mine. I was crushed.

Of all the things that could have happened, this was possibly the one I would never be able to accept. I had lost my baby sister to a drunk driver, and there was no way—no matter how much I was falling in love with him—I would ever be able to look Gavin in the eye again.

I thanked the guys—at least, I thought I did—and ran all the way home. I closed the door behind me and slid all the way to the floor, my head against the cold surface and tears streaming down my cheeks, little rivulets of pain and sorrow. My real man, and first true love, had dissipated like the morning mist over the lake. Just like that, Gavin had gone from hero to villain in my own love story.

***

Gavin

The boot flew across the room in a wide arc and slammed with great aplomb into the wall, narrowly missing Jackson's head as he burst through the open door.

"Fuck, you could have killed me, idiot. What's going on with you?" My friend stared at the heavy boot now lying on the floor, and then back at me.

I mumbled a half-hearted apology from my seated position and focused on my prosthetic foot. A fake heart was a very attractive idea at that moment, since my real one was hurting so bad. I had given my heart away for the first time ever, only to get it stomped on and torn to shreds by the woman I had come to love.

"Dude, you look like shit." Jackson came to sit down next to me on the edge of my bunk. "Did you get any sleep?"

For once, there hadn't been any calls during the night, an almost unheard-of event in a firehouse, but I couldn't sleep. I tossed and turned all night, Ana's beautiful face imprinted inside my eyelids. Why was this happening? What could have possibly happened to make her so mad at me she wouldn't pick up the phone? One minute, she had been next to me, playing with the firehouse's new mascot; the next, she was gone.

"She won't talk to me." The sting of unshed tears burned in my eyes. I hadn't cried in a very long time. In fact, I hadn't even cried when I found out I had lost my leg. Anger, red-hot wrath, had colored my feelings then, but the tears never came. It took a tiny little woman to break me.

Jackson patted my back. "What did you do?"

Thanks, Jacks, for so quickly jumping to the conclusion I did something wrong.

"I'm totally befuckled," I said, refusing to lift my suspiciously moist eyes. "I'm fucked-up and confused. I don't know what to think. Nothing happened. Nothing."

"That's rough, Gavin." Jackson got on his feet and began gathering my discarded clothes from the floor and piling them up on a chair. "Just let it go. Maybe she'll come around."

My head snapped up. "Around? Around what?" My voice was unnecessarily shrill, and I immediately felt guilty for talking to him like that. "Sorry, man. I'm just so messed up."

"Jump in the shower and come have lunch with my wife and me."

It was a nice invite, but I didn't feel like being around two people in love. Watching Jackson and his lovely wife would be like rubbing salt on an open wound.

"Thanks, Jacks, but I think I'm going home to sleep."

After a quick shower, I walked the short distance to my house. As an afterthought, I turned around and dragged myself to the Grind N Crepe instead. I sat in our favorite booth. Yes, Ana and I already had a favorite many things—a coffee shop booth, a song, a show on TV, a movie.

I cradled a hot mug of coffee in my hands and allowed my thoughts to roam free. I wasn't sure how long I sat there, staring into everything and seeing nothing. Emptiness filled my chest where my heart and soul had imploded and bled to death.

"Gavin?" A familiar voice snapped me out of my reverie, and the world came into focus again. Elaine Mathews had slipped into the opposite seat in the booth and stared at me with interest. "Are you all right?

Of all the people I could have met right then, Ana's

mother was not the one I expected or wanted. If her daughter was so mad at me she wouldn't even answer my calls, what would her mom's reaction be?

"You look sick," she said, surprising me with her genuine concern. "Are you here to meet my daughter?"

Hell, Ana hadn't told her either. "Ana is not talking to me." *I sound like a sulking child.* "She's mad about something but won't tell me what."

The gorgeous Mrs. Mathews frowned. "Ana can be very stubborn. Have you asked her?"

I swiped a hand over my face and sighed. "I've called a million times, left her messages, and even went knocking at her door. She refuses to give me the time of day."

"You must have seriously screwed up." Was that a hint of laughter in her voice? I failed to see the humor in all of it, so I scowled. "Don't give me that look, young man. My daughter is a bit defensive when it comes to matters of the heart, but she wouldn't just stop talking to you on a whim. Something must have happened." I shook my head. "Something you said?" I shook it even more emphatically. "Something someone else said?"

That had not occurred to me. Ana had been talking to Alan and Justin right before she took off running. Had they said something about me that made her mad? But what? I had no skeletons in the closet, and was generally well-liked by my coworkers. Maybe I should call the men and ask what they had been talking about with my sweet writer that had made her bolt.

"Are you serious about Ana?" The question took me by surprise, and I almost dropped the mug I had lifted to my lips. "You must be if you're this upset about it."

I might as well come clean. Nothing to lose at that point. "I'm in love with your daughter." I couldn't believe I'd said it out loud. Maybe not to the right person yet, but it was progress. I hoped.

Ana's mother smiled, her well-shaped lips stretching and her eyes glowing. "I knew it. I could tell by the way you looked at her when she wasn't looking. The way my husband used to look at me when we were dating."

"Not anymore?" I bit my tongue. What kind of an idiot was I to ask such a question?

She didn't seem too upset. "No, unfortunately I lost my husband some years ago." I winced. "He's not dead. He left me."

"I'm so sorry."

"He couldn't handle being around us after we lost our youngest daughter." Ana had had a sister? Why had she never mentioned it? "He doted on her—understandably, since she was a sweetheart, smart, and talented. But when she was killed by that drunk driver, he couldn't even look at us. I think we reminded him too much of her."

Interesting that Ana had never once spoken about this. Granted, we hadn't known each other for too long, but this seemed like a rather important detail in her life. Her sister had been killed by a drunk driver—could

118

that be somehow the connection to this whole mess? But how would that make her angry at me?

"Anyway, I hope you can fix things with my girl." Mrs. Mathews stood and offered me her hand. "You're a good, brave man and my daughter deserves nothing less. I didn't move back from Seattle to watch my daughter be miserable. Make it work."

Her tone of voice made me smile as I stood up to shake her hand. "Or what?"

"Or I will hunt you down and make you regret you ever met me." With a wink, she turned around and left me. I believed her.

***

Ana

I had run out of tears hours before. On top of my coffee table, a pile of snotty tissues looked suspiciously like Mount Everest, and the mirror across the way told me raccoons had nothing on me with my mascara-smudged eyes and face. When the bell rang, I ignored it at first, but after ten or more rings, I knew I couldn't anymore.

Delta was at the door, a half-gallon container of dark chocolate ice cream in hand and a worried frown. I threw another tissue into the pile and dragged my feet to the couch where I collapsed into the cushions with a groan.

"Sweetie, you're a mess." *Thank you for stating the*

obvious, my friend. Delta closed the door behind her and set the container on the table in front of me. "We'll need spoons."

Coming back from my kitchen with two large spoons in her hand, my friend sat beside me, shaking a few rogue tissues from the couch onto the floor. "I know you're hurting, but it's no excuse to be a slob." I knew she was trying to be funny, but even Delta couldn't make me laugh. Not when my heart was bleeding. I dropped my head on her shoulder and sobbed. "Oh honey, I hate to see you like this." She patted my back, holding me close to her, and I was reminded of another time when she did the same. The memory made me cry even more.

"He killed someone, Delta." My voice was thick with emotion and laced with anger. "How can I look at him now? You know how I feel about drunk drivers." Better than almost anyone—even my mom.

"I know, sweetie. But are you sure?" I snapped my head up to look at her and sniffled. She shrugged apologetically. "Are you certain that's what happened? I mean, he doesn't hit me as the kind to get behind the wheel drunk. Everyone sings his praises—"

I didn't mean to sound so irate, but my heart wouldn't be controlled. I loved a man who was by all definitions the same type of criminal who had killed my sister all those years ago. It made me very angry.

"I know what his friends said. His mentor, some guy called Bill, was killed in that accident. I checked the newspapers from back then and they all said the same thing; the accident was caused by too much alcohol." The words flew out of my mouth hot as flames. "I hate him. I truly hate him."

Delta drew me to her again, her familiar presence giving me a measure of comfort. "No, you don't. That's the problem—you're in love with him."

How does a guy drop from a pedestal reserved for heroes to a dungeon for lowlives within a couple hours? Everybody claimed he had saved numerous lives at his job—a man who didn't let a little thing like a missing limb stop him from venturing to the site of a raging fire. How could that same man be a murderer? Yes, in my book, anyone who sat behind the wheel of a car and drove it drunk was no better than the one who picked up a gun with the intention of shooting someone. He was a murderer like the felon who had mowed down my beautiful, smart little sister as she was coming home from school—my sweet, full of potential baby sister who wanted to be a ballerina and a scientist. Her graduation had been only one week away. Instead, we attended her funeral that day.

"Has he been calling?"

I blew my nose loudly and looked at her from the corner of my eye.

"He has, hasn't he?" Delta sighed and removed the lid from the ice-cream container. "You should talk to him."

I cackled like the old hag I felt. "Talk to him?

Are you fucking serious?"

"You need some closure." She sounded so rational, so calm, I wanted to slap her. "If you don't, you'll be hanging on to this heartache for years, like you did with Rick."

Rick, the suave singer who had bewitched me into marrying him five short months after we met, and with whom I had nothing in common. The same Rick who had hopped in some groupie's bed before we celebrated our first anniversary. The same asshole who ripped my romantic heart to shreds, the one I just recently had begun to piece together again.

"You know I'm right." I hated when she was the sane one in our relationship. "You have to do it. And sooner rather than later."

Delta handed me a spoon and we dug into the ice cream with gusto. I'd be on a diet of Tums the next day, but that sugary, fatty treat was a balm to the soul.

"Do you want me to stay?" She knew me too well.

My lower lip quivered. "Will you?"

Delta smiled, a bit of chocolate ice cream dripping from the corner of her lips. "Of course. I love you, romantic fool."

I made a face, a tiny giggle escaping my lips. "Thank you. You may want to clean your mouth."

Delta puckered her dirty lips. "Does my mouth look like a baby butt?"

"Ewww, that's disgusting, Delta." It was like old times—me being a sensitive idiot and Delta being the goofball who always made me laugh.

"Made you laugh, didn't I?"

I fell into her arms, sobbing and laughing all at the same time, snot flowing freely from my nose and onto her lovely black sweater. Delta would kill me as soon as I was recovered from my broken heart, but for now she allowed it—no, she welcomed it, rubbing circles on my heaving back and cooing like a turtledove.

Despite the hurt, I slept like a baby that night, curled into a ball on the couch under my fluffiest blanket and only half-aware of my best friend's presence next to me. I couldn't be sure what I dreamed of, but I woke up with wet cheeks and the vivid taste of Gavin on my slobbery lips. The smell of cinnamon rolls caressed my nose and inspired me to open my heavy eyelids to face daylight.

"Well, welcome back to the land of the living and awake, my pretty." Delta, wearing one of my giant T-shirts and *Frozen* slippers, was standing by the stove with a spatula in her hand. "Got some sweet buns here. Just follow the scent."

As much as I wanted to go back to sleep, the smell was too tantalizing for me to resist. I sat up and dragged myself to the kitchen, blowing loose strands of my hair away from my nose and my eyes.

"You're evil." My throat was dry and scratchy. I plopped myself on a chair and crossed my arms on top of the table. "I'll be as fat as a cow and you'll have to roll me down the hill."

Delta slid a bun onto a plate and placed it in front of me. "Stop your bellyaching and eat up. Sugar is good for a broken heart."

After devouring two whole rolls and gulping down a huge glass of milk, closely followed by a mug of dark roasted coffee, I took a shower and dressed in my oldest and most comfortable yoga pants, paired up with a light striped hoodie. I wasn't going anywhere. Not now, maybe never. I was going to sit down and bleed into my laptop—heart, guts, and soul—until I had no blood left.

Heroes and Saints

Gavin

The alarm blared through the firehouse, waking every man and woman on duty. I was already awake, tormented by the same dreams I'd been having since Ana inexplicably built a wall around her to keep me out. She haunted every thought, every dream.

I sat up and put on the rest of my uniform before running toward the fire truck. While the other men quickly filtered in through the door to the station's living quarters, I turned on the engine's lights and let it idle until everyone was in the cab.

Through my helmet's intercom, I heard Jackson's voice giving us information about the incident we were heading to, but I couldn't focus. I hadn't slept properly in a long time. I shook my head and made myself pay attention to the instructions. It wouldn't be fair to my unit or possible victims if I was distracted enough not to function at 100 percent.

As soon as I heard the address, I mapped the way in my head as I always did, and turned on the first street to the right.

"Gas leak near a small shopping strip," Jackson said. I hated those more than any others, because it normally affected multiple buildings at the same time. Gas was one of the things in my line of work that scared me the most because of its unpredictability and potential danger—greater possibility of explosions and fatalities.

Jackson jumped out of the truck even before it stopped completely, rushing straight to where the leak had been reported to be—a hole made by a contractor the evening before. As we staged Engine 1 and Ladder 2 as far from the leak as we deemed safe, Jackson came running back.

"Masks at the ready and secure the perimeter," he yelled. "No one comes near. I can hear the gas leak."

My team put their masks on while I dialed the number for the utility company. The gas source had to be cut off immediately.

While my men went from door to door making sure they were empty, I watched a little forlornly from the safety of the fire engine. At moments like this, I wished I could be whole again and be up front, side by side with the others, instead of watching all the action from a distance. I kept my eyes on my friend, Jackson, who with his usual speed and efficiency walked from one place to another with the gas monitors, taking readings. He signaled us that the readings were high and we should stay away.

That's when I saw it—a shiny, almost sparkling reddish glow that could be nothing but some type of electrical short. The place was going to blow and my friend was at the epicenter of the explosion. I stopped thinking rationally and ran as fast as my prosthetic leg would allow me with only one thought in my head—get him out of there quick.

Jackson didn't see me coming as I tackled him and tried to push him away from the gas leak and the ominous spark. We didn't go far. A loud noise pierced my eardrums, and I flew off the ground high enough I could see the top of the white oak tree in the parking lot. My lungs couldn't take in any air under the pressure of the explosion, and I thought I was going to die right then. I hit the ground at the same time as many other things that had been sent flying in the blast. Jackson fell just a few yards away from me. He wasn't moving. Desperate to make sure he was okay, I tried to go to him but I still couldn't breathe.

Just as I was finally able to take a breath—however shallow—something heavy fell on my back, crushing me again. The pain was indescribable. I had very little memory of how I'd felt or even what had happened during the car accident all those years ago. There must have been a lot of pain, but I couldn't recall any of it. Nothing like this.

Oh my God. I'm going to die.

My ears were ringing from the explosion, but I heard the Mayday, clear as crystal, coming through my helmet's speaker. "Two men down, two men down."

The heat suddenly scorching my sides told me the structure was on fire. I wasn't close enough to get burned, but big flaming chunks of the building were falling all around me. I was screwed if one of them fell on me. I tried to crawl to Jackson again, but my legs weren't cooperating and neither were my burning lungs. *Am I on fire?*

"Don't move, Gavin." The order came from nearby, muffled by a face piece. "Don't budge."

I had no intention of moving by then. Every little attempt at motion made my body convulse in excruciating pain. I was quickly fading out from the lack of oxygen. I was going to die, and I'd never had the chance to apologize for whatever it was I had done to my Ana. I'd never have the chance to tell her how much I loved her.

"Incoming!" I heard it before I felt it. A sudden, fierce explosion against the back of my head. I had a strange moment of clarity where the world came back into clear focus before total and utter darkness enveloped and took me under.

***

Ana

The whiteness of the screen goaded me. *"Come on, write something on me. I dare you."* I couldn't. I had been staring at the laptop screen for over an hour and hadn't managed a single word. My muse had left me. My brain cells had died and left nothing but emptiness in their place.

I rubbed my forehead in despair. I had a deadline coming up and I wasn't even halfway done with this story. "I hate this!" The truth was, I couldn't take my mind off Gavin. If my rational side said there was no way a relationship with a drunk driver would ever work, my heart kept pulling me the other way. I loved the guy. Really, truly, and completely. I hated myself for it, but a heart cannot be denied.

The phone rang and I stretched across the table to get it. The caller ID told me it was an unknown local number. Curious—and bored—I picked up.

"Ms. Mathews?" The voice was familiar, but I couldn't place it. "This is Alan from the firehouse."

Was Gavin using his friends to reach me? "I don't want to talk to Gavin. Tell him—"

He interrupted me. "No, he didn't ask me to call you. I just thought you'd want to know."

"Know what?" My curiosity was piqued.

"There's been an accident." My heart plummeted. Memories of another call a few years ago came flooding back to me. Those were the same words I heard when they first called about my sister. "Gavin is in the hospital."

I wasn't sure what happened next. I remembered running out my door and getting into a taxi—had I called it? The drive to the hospital was a blur of fear and anger burning in my heart at the same time. Fear of losing the man I loved, and anger for what he had done. How could you love someone while hating what he was?

Several men from Gavin's unit were gathered in the hospital ER lobby, most still in their pants and tunics, soot staining their faces. A couple of them had bleeding scratches, and they all had wild stares, as if they had seen something they'd rather forget. I recognized Alan and Justin milling around, twisting their hands and staring at the floor. In a semidaze, I sped toward them, a sob caught in my throat.

"What happened? Is he—?" I couldn't finish the thought, realizing I couldn't even imagine my fireman dead. "How is he?" I swallowed my tears for fear of losing control and drowning in my own grief.

Alan looked up first, a flash of recognition crossing his eyes. "Ms. Mathews, you're here." *Of course, I am here. Where else would I be?* Oh, right, I hadn't spoken to Gavin in a while. "Gavin was caught in a gas explosion with Jackson." For the first time, I noticed Jackson's absence from the room.

Alan held my arm just below my elbow and led me to a seat nearby. "How? What the hell happened? Is he alive?"

"They're both hurt but alive." I exhaled, relief softening my muscles, which had been wound tighter than a two-dollar watch. "Thanks to Gavin."

My breath caught. "What do you mean?" Had Gavin caused this incident as well?

Alan sat next to me. "If it weren't for him getting Jackson away from the gas leak at the right moment, Jacks would have been dead."

My lips stretched into a smile. That was the Gavin I knew and loved. Not the drunkard who stupidly drove a car and his friend into a tree. "He saved Jackson?" My voice shrank with the emotion that filled my heart.

The young man nodded. "He sure did. At great risk to himself." My eyebrows rose in question. "He could have died along with Jacks."

Enough talk. I needed to see him for myself. Make sure he was indeed alive and reasonably safe and sound. "When can I see him?"

Justin approached, exhaustion and worry visible in the folds under his eyes. "The doctors are still removing shrapnel from him. He also had a nasty encounter with a piece of concrete. He was unconscious when we got him to the hospital."

Determined to see him, I marched to the check-in counter. "Excuse me, my boyfriend is one of the firemen who got hurt." Surprised I had called Gavin my boyfriend, I blinked a few times. "Can I see him?"

"He's in treatment," the receptionist said. "We'll let you in as soon as he's done."

Reluctantly I sat down next to Alan, who still seemed a little dazed. He was very young, and I suddenly wondered if this was his first time on a call that led to injury. My maternal instincts—which I didn't know I had—kicked in and I wrapped my hand around his shoulder, pulling him to me in what I hoped was a comforting gesture. He yielded to my gentle pull and we sat together, deriving some solace from each other's heat.

I may have dozed off, or maybe I just went to my "happy place." When I finally heard my name called, I jumped to my feet, almost toppling poor Alan—still leaning on me—to the floor.

The nurse took me through a maze of hospital corridors and into a small room in the ICU where my beloved fireman was stretched on a bed, half-covered by white blankets and with wires connected to several parts of his body. *What have you done to yourself, Gavin?* I entered the room quietly, tiptoeing to his bedside.

"He's still unconscious." I had forgotten the nurse behind me and I jerked in surprise. "He took a nasty hit to the head. We gave him some sedatives for the pain. There was a lot of shrapnel in him, and some minor burns."

I sighed, my chest still constricted in fear. "But he'll be all right—"

The nurse nodded. "Yes, he will be perfectly okay. He just needs to rest, get lots of fluids, and allow his body to heal." A wide smile stretched her lips. "This one is a tough cookie. I still remember him from when he lost his leg."

My stomach churned and somersaulted. I didn't want to hear about his accident right now. I wanted to focus on my love for him, not the reasons why we could never be together. At least until he was well and I could hate him again. Except I could never hate him, not completely.

"You can stay here until he wakes up if you like. I'm sure he'll be happy to see you."

After the nurse left the room, the silence surrounded me, interrupted regularly by the beeps of the heart monitor. I sat and watched my man, looking vulnerable and beautiful, his face covered in bloody cuts, a bandage around his head and one of his arms. His deliciously sexy lips sported an ugly cut and I yearned to soothe it with my kisses. What a fool I was. Head over heels in love with a man I could never, ever be with. The knowledge he had killed someone because of the same recklessness and disregard for others that had taken my young sister away from me would always be a wall between us. *Us* was not to be.

***

Gavin

Stupid beeping. How can anyone sleep with that racket?

I could see faint light through the slits of my eyes, and it took me a while to realize where I was. What had they given me? I felt as if I'd had way too much to drink the night before. I tried to open my eyes, but the eyelids were heavy as lead, and I belatedly realized the bump on my head was not going to make it easy to move either.

"Fuck!" Sad that my first word after this ordeal was a profanity, but I thought the pain in the back of my head and the fact that I could have died justified it well enough.

I felt, rather than saw, movement at the side of my bed, and a soft touch on my shoulder. *An angel?* I managed to crack an eye open and saw her. Better than any angel—my Ana was standing right next to me.

"Careful. Don't move too much, Gavin." Aw, she was concerned about my well-being. Maybe there was hope for us after all. "You just went through a lot." Her voice caught a little and I immediately wanted to hug and comfort her.

"I'm okay. Just sore." Well, maybe a little more than just sore. My arm hurt like hell and my head was pounding. I tried to open my eyes again with moderate success. I could see her clearly now, her hand still gingerly touching my shoulder as if afraid she would hurt me. My beautiful Ana. My heart melted a little. "Are *you* all right? Haven't heard from you in a while." I had to ask.

"I'm fine." She didn't want to talk about it; that

much was obvious as her arm stiffened and her eyes dropped. "You could have died, you know."

"It's my job. I may not have a lot of chances to be in the thick of things with my disability and all, but it's still in my job description." I hoped she couldn't hear the bitterness in my voice. "Besides, it was my best friend out there. I was the closest to him at the time—shit! How is he? Did he make it?"

In my sudden panic, I moved too quickly and a sharp pain pierced through my skull. I dropped my head back on the pillow and closed my eyes. *Shit, shit, shit.*

Ana pressed me gently against the bed, afraid I was going to try and sit up again. "He's fine. You saved his life. He suffered some minor burns and scratches. In fact, he's in better shape than you." Her voice trembled. "You're the hero—this time."

"I'm no hero," I protested. Then I realized what she had said. "What do you mean, this time?"

She pulled up a chair and sat at my bedside, leaving an emptiness on my shoulder. "Never mind. The important thing is that both you and Jackson are okay."

Silence fell. What a strange thing for her to say. I wanted to inquire further, but I was so happy she was there I didn't want to taint the moment with a potential argument.

"Thank you."

I love you.

"For what?" she asked.

Do you love me too?

"For coming. For being here when I woke up."
My hand searched for hers, but to no avail. She was
keeping her hands selfishly on her lap, away from
mine. "I can't tell you how happy I was to see your
face when I opened my eyes. I miss you."

Tell her already.

"Alan called me. I was worried." Her eyes avoided
mine. What was going on?

"Are you mad at me?" There, it was out. "I mean,
you haven't answered my phone calls or come
around—obviously, there is something going on. What
is it? What have I done?"

She moved as if to stand up. Risking another
stabbing pain, I reached out and stopped her.

"I should go, Gavin. I have a deadline." Feeble
excuses to cover up whatever it was bothering her.
Why wouldn't she just tell me? I was clueless. How
could I defend myself when I didn't know what I was
being accused of?

"No, please stay. Please." My head was about
to explode, but that was nothing compared to the
gathering pain in my heart. I couldn't lose her. "Ana, I
don't know why you're mad at me, but I'm sure we can
talk it over. It can't be so bad that we can't at least try
to solve it. Please, Ana, I'm begging you."

"I can't talk about it." Not helping. "Maybe someday.
I'll stay for now and keep you company." She sat back
on the chair and ventured a glance at me. Her eyes
were puffy and rimmed in red. I wasn't sure whether to

be happy she was concerned about me enough to cry, or worried that those were tears of anger.

A couple of the guys picked that moment to come in the room. "Hey, here's the hero, looking no worse for the wear." They were still wearing their uniforms. They hadn't left the hospital yet. "How are you feeling, man?"

They pulled a couple chairs over and retold the story of my heroic rescue over and over again, each time adding details I had no recollection of. By the time they were finished, I had been elevated to the status of a saint. I laughed at their lack of factual memory, and they assured me they remembered it all too well.

"Fuck, dude. Jackson and you flew up like two rockets on the Fourth of July. It's a miracle you guys didn't break any bones," one of them said with a boisterous chuckle.

"Or die, for that matter," the other one added unhelpfully. I glanced at Ana, whose face had gone from pale to transparent as the story rolled off my men's embellishing tongues. I longed to take her in my arms and kiss her until she relaxed against me.

"Nobody died and we weren't even in any real danger." I threw a pointed glance at them, hoping they would take the hint that I didn't want to worry Ana any more than she was already.

"Stop being so fucking humble, man. That explosion could have killed you both. Easily." My telepathic gifts were not working. I rolled my eyes, giving up on trying to curb their enthusiasm about events.

For the next hour or so, there was a constant flow of people coming in and out through my room door, each time with some version of the same story. I watched Ana as she became quieter and paler with each account, but I couldn't do anything about it.

When the last person finally left, Ana stood up as well. "I have to go. You need your rest."

This time I was able to reach out for her hand and hold it. "No, wait. There is something I need to tell you."

"You can tell me another time." She pulled her hand away from mine, but I held it firmly.

"Please, sit for a second." I must have sounded desperate, because she did, her hand still inside mine and a noticeable quiver on her lips.

"What's so urgent that it can't wait until tomorrow?"

I can't be sure you'll be back.

I took a deep breath and exhaled slowly. Still holding her hand, I raised my eyes to hers and licked my lips. This was a first for me and I wanted to be sure I said it the right way.

When nothing came out of my mouth, she fidgeted in her seat, her hand trembling. "Well? What is it, Gavin?"

In the end, I figured simplicity was probably the way to go. "I love you, Ana Mathews."

I was not sure what to expect, but the frightened frown on Ana's face was not it.

Truth and Misunderstandings

Ana

"I don't get it." Delta stabbed the cupcake with gusto. "He tells you he loves you and you—let me get this straight—you walk away? Why?" Another stab, and the once beautifully decorated cake looked like the victim of a mudslide, the chocolate icing running down the cracks of the demolished confection. "You're so obviously in love with this guy. I don't get you."

My respect for everything beautiful made me cringe at the sight of her cupcake abuse. "I do love him. A lot." So much, my heart couldn't contain it all and it threatened to spill over. "But I'm also a realist, and I know that the fact he was a drunk driver who killed someone will be a nasty monster of a thing between the two of us. It will emerge from the background every time we have a fight or I need something to blame him for. It wouldn't work."

With a mouth full of chocolate cake, Delta glanced at me and chewed silently for a moment. "You're an idiot."

I flinched. As used as I was to my friend's bluntness, I didn't expect that kind of reaction from her. "Why do you say that? I'm just preventing a lot of heartache for both me and Gavin."

Delta wiped her mouth with the napkin and turned her body slightly toward me. "Really? So, you're telling me that breaking off this thing between you right now won't cause you or him any pain. Is that right?"

My mouth had gone desert dry. "No, it will hurt. Lots." Like a festering wound that wouldn't heal.

"If it will hurt that much breaking up now, doesn't that defeat the purpose of *not* getting into a relationship with him?" She could be way too sensible and logical sometimes. "Wouldn't it make more sense to talk to him about it and establish whether he still drinks too much? I mean, we all have done pretty stupid things in our youth."

"But his *stupid thing* cost someone else's life. How do you atone for that?" Would I ever be able to forgive the man who had killed my sister? I didn't think so. Granted, he was unrepentant and had even tried to sue my mother for undue stress after the judge had let him go with only a slap on the wrist. Gavin had lost a leg and turned his life around completely, as far as I could tell.

I'm so confused.

"Listen, before you decide to throw the love of your life away with the trash, talk to him. See what he has to say for himself."

She had a point. Ever since the gas explosion a couple days ago, I had been less determined about calling it quits and more inclined to see how things worked out. *Be careful what you wish for*. I had been looking for a real man, and now that I had one, I was having trouble accepting his flaws. What kind of human being did that make me?

I waited all day, puttering around the house, sporadically sitting with my laptop and writing a bit more of the novel-that-wouldn't-be. Not that time was helpful. The more I thought about it, the more confused I became. Night had already fallen when I finally made the decision to go to his house and confront him about it.

He had been released from the hospital the day after the incident. I hadn't been to see him, but the neighborhood friendly gossipers—Alan and Justin—had kept me abreast of every little development. Gavin was still sore and off duty, but healing quickly. They had also felt compelled to share that their bionic friend—as they liked to call him—missed me something awful and was a mere shadow of his normal self as a result. Who knew that the two young firemen were romantics at heart?

My small Yaris had trouble starting after such a long time in the garage without use. I didn't drive often since

I normally didn't go far from home. My introvert self was perfectly happy walking around the neighborhood or taking rides from friends when I did indeed have to go someplace to where walking was not an option. My characters were well traveled, but I had only traveled within the pages of books or through movies and TV shows. After getting married, my husband had taken me on a honeymoon to Florida, but that was the extent of my traveling life.

I parked out in the street and then stood by the curb, frowning at the awful job I had done. The back tire of my car was practically over the curb while the front end stuck out into the street, as if giving every passerby the finger. I shook my head and turned around, walking away quickly before I felt the pull to perfect my parking job.

The door buzzed after I rang the bell. I climbed the stairs to his floor, and then stood like an idiot, facing the door and willing myself to knock. *Déjà vu.*

Like the first time I had done this, the door suddenly opened, leaving me with my fist propped up and my eyes wide in surprise. Gavin, head and arm still bandaged, stood there—all six-odd feet of him, shirtless and toned. My girly bits reacted before I could. The heat that the sight of him produced in me climbed from my lower body to my face in a furious wave. I lowered my fist and bit my lower lip, trying to calm down my fast-beating heart without much success.

"Ana." His sexy, gruff voice melted something

inside of me, and I threw myself unwisely into his arms. "Ouch. I'm a little tender." His soft chuckle belied his words as his arms went around me.

"Can we talk?" My voice, muffled against his chest, surprised me, as if it belonged to someone else.

Still within the cocoon of his arms, I kicked the door closed behind me and walked with him to the living room. His lips brushed the top of my head, and my knees grew weak. *Focus, woman.*

"Not that I'm complaining, but why are you here?"

Gavin led us to the sofa and I dropped into the soft cushions, never once letting go. Suddenly, I was afraid of losing him. Afraid I would blink and he'd be gone.

"I love you." Every intention of talking things over, of asking him about his accident, flew out of my mind. All I could think was of how much I loved him, this flesh and bone man, as real and beautiful as the rising sun. My real man.

Gavin's breath caught and his eyes widened just enough to betray his surprise. "You—what?"

I covered his cheeks with my hands and looked him straight in the eyes. "I. Love. You."

I brought my lips to his and drowned in his flavor. I would cross the questions bridge later. But at that moment, I realized that living without him would be more unbearable than knowing what he had done. Whoever he had been then was not who he was now. The man kissing me as if there was no tomorrow was a hero, someone who didn't hesitate to jump into danger to save a friend. Not someone who would drive intoxicated and kill a mentor.

"I love you too." I felt the words as he moved his lips over mine and I caught on fire. Hell and brimstone wouldn't stop me from loving him fully, body and soul.

***

Gavin

Clothing items flew in great, graceful arcs, falling scattered to the wooden floor around us in a colorful downpour of sorts. In the end, Ana and I stood naked in the middle of my living room, taking each other in, breathing ragged in anticipation.

Still finding it hard to believe she was really there, beautiful flesh and bone illuminated by the muted light, I reached out to touch her. I cupped her breast and shivered as she moaned gently and leaned against my hand. I followed my hand with my lips, coaxing more whimpering from her. Anxious to be inside her, I hooked an arm around her waist and lifted her up, her legs knotted behind my hips. She vibrated under my touch—her softness against my hardness, her gentle curves merging with the ridges of my muscles.

"I need you." I kissed her along the earlobe and squeezed her tighter against me. My hands were under her small, firm bottom, supporting her weight, hugging her closer and closer to me. Her body radiated heat into mine. "I love you so much it's crazy."

We stumbled across the room, her arms wrapped around my neck, mouths fused in a thirsty kiss that wouldn't be quenched. In the room, we dropped together onto the bed. I raised myself on my arms, hovering above her, to have another glance at her beauty. She reached down between us and caressed me until I was hard as a rock and shaking with yearning.

"Can't wait anymore." Her voice, husky with desire, was all the invitation I needed. I jumped out of bed, hopped to where I kept my condoms, and was back before she knew I was gone. I fumbled with the packet until she took it away from me, ripped it open, and rolled it maddeningly slowly over me. "Now, we're ready." She licked her lips and I was lost.

Our connected bodies moved together in a frantic game of to-and-fro, punctuated by our own groans of pleasure until we both reached nirvana and collapsed in each other's arms, spent and sated. I had never been one for poetry or philosophy, but at that moment for some strange reason, a quote from Rumi came to mind: "Happy is the moment we sit together, with two forms, with two faces, yet one soul. You and I." I loved this woman more than I had ever loved anyone or anything.

We must have slept, because the next thing I knew, the weak rays of the morning sun were seeping through the cracks in the blinds, giving my sweet Ana an otherworldly glow. She was still entwined in my arms, my body molding hers, my mouth resting in the crook of her graceful neck. I didn't want to move. I wanted to stay like that forever, comfortable and secure in her love, our bodies perfectly matched like two pieces of a puzzle.

Unfortunately, I needed to use the bathroom. Badly. As stealthily as I could, I pulled my arm from underneath her and retreated from her lovely warm body, feeling suddenly empty. She moved and whimpered quietly in protest, but didn't wake up. Maybe I would be able to crawl into bed with her afterward.

When I returned from my bathroom mission, I found her lying on her side, head resting on one hand and a wicked smile on her lips. She scanned me from my toes to the top of my head with an appreciative wink of the eye.

"You're very yummy."

High praise indeed coming from a woman who created hot guys who only lived in the imaginations of women—and some guys. If I scored that high on her scale, she must be really in love with me. My mechanical leg did not add any sexiness to my body. I smiled back at her and, playing her game, I leaned against the wall, striking what I thought may be a sexy pose.

She burst out laughing.

"That hurts my fragile ego, woman." It didn't. I loved her laughter—the way her giggles bubbled up her throat and fell off her lips like crystals, clinking against each other in a symphony of rings and jingles.

I ran to the bed and threw myself on top, falling right next to her. Her mouth descended on mine, her tongue playing along the edges of my lips before seeking mine. Was it possible I loved her more today than last night?

I wrapped her in my arms, enjoying every bit of bodily contact. I was hard again and very willing to go another round of loving, but Ana seemed to have other ideas. She cuddled against my chest, her dark hair tickling me as she butterfly-kissed me.

"I want you to know I will always love you." *Me too.* "I will never allow your past to get between us, I promise." *That* was unexpected.

"What do you mean?" I had no idea what she was talking about. My past? What past? *Does she mean the string of meaningless hookups throughout the years?* I was not that different from other guys my age, so how did that make a *past*?

"Whatever you may have done in the past, I won't let it come between us. However hard it is for me to accept it." Odd. Very odd indeed.

"You know that all those girls I dated were never serious, right?" She had never brought my romantic past up before. Why now?

"I don't mean that, Gavin." Her hand was drawing imaginary circles over my chest, raising goose bumps. "I don't care about who you dated before. God, I was married." *Then what?* "I mean the accident."

The accident? Why would that come between us?

Is she talking about my prosthetic leg? "Does the leg bother you that much that you think it will get in the way of us?"

Her head snapped up, her chin now digging into my chest and her eyes burning on mine. "Of course not. Why would I care about your leg?"

"You said my accident. How can my accident get in the way?" I was so confused I thought for a moment the meds they gave me for the pain may still be having their weird effect on me.

"I'm talking about you driving that car the night of the accident." *What?*

"I wasn't driving the car." Her eyes became round as saucers. "I should have never gotten into that car, but I thought I could convince Bill not to drive when he was so fucking drunk. I was wrong." Her mouth agape, Ana paled. "He drove anyway, and about killed me along with himself." This conversation was more effective than a cold shower. Images of that night invaded my mind and I shook my head in an attempt to dispel them.

In a totally unexpected move, Ana jumped up to her knees and threw her arms up in the air. "Yay! Oh my God, I'm so happy."

Shit. Those meds are doing a number on me.

"You're happy Bill crashed that car, killing himself and making me disabled for the rest of my life?"

Ana threw herself on top of me, her mouth crushing against mine. Her breasts, jammed against my chest, made me swell again, and I wiggled under her in some discomfort. "Dummy. I love you." *Okay, she loves dumb guys. Not sure how to react to that.* "I'm happy you weren't the one driving that night. I thought—oh shit, I thought you had killed your mentor."

Cold shower effect again. Man, this conversation was putting my body through the wringer.

"You thought I was the driver? That I had driven drunk and crashed the car?"

"Yes, and I've been having such a hard time coming to terms with that." Her chin quivered, and I hugged her tighter against me. "You know, my sister was killed by a drunk driver. I wasn't sure I could love you and accept the fact you had done the same to somebody else."

A light bulb went on inside my brain. "Is that why you're mad at me?" I twisted my head so I could look at her face. "Why didn't you tell me?"

"Because I'm so freaking dumb. I was scared of what excuses you may come up with." A rogue tear rolled down her cheek, and I wiped it with my thumb. "It would be even worse if you tried to justify what you—what I thought you did."

"Oh, baby, we're both fools. I should have told you my story a long time ago." We would have avoided so many misunderstandings. "It always brings so many bad memories, I— It's hard to talk about it. That's all."

We held each other in silence for a while, enjoying each other's heat, until my body began misbehaving again.

Ana giggled. "Really? Now?"

I shrugged. "I'm not in control here, duckling. My body knows what it wants, and apparently it wants you again."

She laughed and feathered her fingers down my middle teasingly. "Who am I to argue with this bionic body of yours?"

I groaned. "Not you too." But I didn't care. As soon as her mouth came down on me, I forgot the world around us existed. It was just Ana and me starring in this epic romance of ours.

***

Ana

His muscles bulged from the short sleeves of his tight T-shirt, and she fanned herself, suddenly feeling the flames of desire licking at her toes. He was a god, all tattooed muscle. She quivered in anticipation of what those big hands of his were about to do to her. Hard to believe he was hers.

Ana laughed. She had decided she didn't need to write about a real man, considering she had one. A man who fulfilled all her fantasies and desires. She was an ordinary woman with simple needs and dreams. Being able to make love to Gavin every night and walk hand in hand with him down the street was a dream come true. One she was not willing to share even with her faithful and beloved readers.

Let the readers find their own real men. In the meantime, she would give them the stuff they loved and craved. The very unreal—and so unlike what she considered sexy—men of romantic fantasies, while she would enjoy every beautiful minute she had with her fireman hero. Her real man.

<<<<>>>

Acknowledgments

My grandfather was a volunteer fireman in Portugal, a lifetime ago. Our house was right by the fire station and we were often startled by the loud sirens calling all volunteers to the firehouse in the wee hours of the night. Avô Albuquerque was more of what I like to call—since I don't know the real term—a "house fireman". He didn't actually go to the site of the event, but helped the others get prepared and took care of things while they were gone. Still, I remember watching through the window as many of the local men ran, often still in their pajamas, to report to duty at the fire station in the middle of the night. Selfless people willing to risk everything for no pay.

This year many firefighters, brave men and women, risked and even lost their lives trying to protect others from the flames. My tiny country, Portugal, was ravaged by fires this summer. Thousands of firefighters worked nonstop for days trying to save lives and the forests of the nation. Many, many thanks for your service.

And to all who, faced with terrible odds and life shattering events, never stop trying, never give up, I salute you. You're an inspiration.

Grind N Crepe, your crepes rock! Food is always great inspiration for my stories. Even more when coffee is involved.

Thank you, Mom, Dad, and sis for believing in me even when I didn't. Love you.

And a big thank you to my publisher, editors, and amazing beta readers. You're amazing and I couldn't have done it without you.

About the Author

Natalina wrote her first romance in collaboration with her best friend at the age of 13. Since then she has ventured into other genres, but romance is first and foremost in almost everything she writes. Her novel, We Will Always Have the Closet, is her first published romance.

After earning a degree in tourism and foreign languages, she worked as a tourist guide in her native country, Portugal, for a short time before moving to the United States. She's lived in three continents and a few islands, and her knack for languages and linguistics led her to a master's degree in education. She lives in Virginia where she has taught English as a second language to elementary school children for more years than she cares to admit.

Natalina doesn't believe you can have too many books or too much coffee. Art and dance make her happy and she is pretty sure she could survive on lobster and bananas alone. When she is not writing or stressing over lesson plans, she shares her life with her husband and two adult sons.

You can reach out to Natalina at the following places:

FACEBOOK: WWW.FACEBOOK.COM/AUTHORNATALINAREIS
WEBSITE: WWW.CATARINADEOBIDOS.WORDPRESS.COM
TWITTER: WWW.TWITTER.COM/TICHAB

About the Publisher

Hot Tree Publishing opened its doors in 2015 with an aspiration to bring quality fiction to the world of readers. With the initial focus on romance and a wide spread of romance sub-genres, we envision opening up to alternative genres in the near future.

Firmly seated in the industry as a leading editing provider to independent authors and small publishing houses, Hot Tree Publishing is the sister company to Hot Tree Editing, founded in 2012. Having established in-house editing and promotions, plus having a well-respected market presence, Hot Tree Publishing endeavors to be a leader in bringing quality stories to the world of readers.

Interested in discovering more amazing reads brought to you by Hot Tree Publishing? Head over to the website for more:

WWW.HOTTREEPUBLISHING.COM

CPSIA information can be obtained
at www.ICGtesting.com
Printed in the USA
BVOW06s0818020218
506998BV00005B/1/P